E:

CW0406688

V

Exit

A Romanian Story

———◆———

RICHARD WAGNER

Translated by
Quintin Hoare

VERSO

London · New York

First published as *Ausreiseantrag* by Luchterhand Literaturverlag 1988
English translation published by Verso 1990
© 1988 Luchterhand Literaturverlag GmbH
Translation © Quintin Hoare 1990

Verso
UK: 6 Meard Street, London W1V 3HR
USA: 29 West 35th Street, New York, NY 10001–2291

Verso is the imprint of New Left Books

British Library Cataloguing in Publication Data
Wagner, Richard, *1952–*
Exit : a Romanian story.
I. Title II. Ausreiseantrag, *English*
833.914

ISBN 0-86091-243-4
ISBN 0-86091-510-7 Pbk

US Library of Congress Cataloging in Publication Data
Wagner, Richard, 1952-
[Ausreiseantrag, English]
Exit : a Romanian story / Richard Wagner :
translated by Quintin Hoare.
p.   cm.
Translation of : Ausreiseantrag.
ISBN 0-86091-243-4. – ISBN 0-86091-510-7 (pbk.)
PT2685.A4446A9413   1990
833'.914—dc20

Typeset by Textflow Services Ltd., Belfast, N. Ireland
Printed in Great Britain by Bookcraft (Bath) Ltd.

PREFACE

After three years, I'm back in the city of Temesvar.* When I left, I saw it as goodbye for ever. Every place I went into, I was going into for the last time. Every street where I lingered, I was there for the last time. Every glance was the last glance, every gesture a last gesture. My despair about the situation in the country was so great that I couldn't conceive of returning. That was in the winter of 1987. I sat in the apartment that would be ours for just a few more weeks and worked on a story. It was meant to illustrate why leaving was the only possible option. The story was published a year ago in the Federal Republic of Germany under the title *Ausreiseantrag*, and is published here as *Exit*.

In Romania, I belonged to the German minority, the Swabians of the Banat. The Banat is situated in the southwest of the country, where Romanian national territory converges with that of Hungary and Yugoslavia. From the seventies on, there was an agreement between Ceausescu and the Federal government on 'reuniting families', in the context of which the Federal government paid bounty for

---

* Temesvar, chief town of the Banat, has a mixed population of Hungarians, Romanians, Germans, Serbs, etc. Traditionally known abroad by this, its Hungarian name, it has figured prominently in the world's press recently under its Romanian name, Timisoara.

emigrants at so much per head. In the dictator's eyes, these people had for years been simply a welcome means of procuring hard currency. Anyone who could leave the country did so, and by the end many were abandoning it like a sinking ship.

It's January 1990 and, for the first time, I'm back in the places of my former life. Steps, gestures, words. They have a tinge of unreality. I cannot yet grasp it: the dictator is dead. Three years are a short time; three years are a long time. I'm a visitor.

The Romanian people has learnt two new words in these days: 'genocide' and 'terrorist'. It was for genocide that the Ceausescus were sentenced to death and executed. People were pleased about it, but for most of them it happened too quickly. 'Their skin should have been taken off in strips', says an elderly woman. 'They didn't suffer enough', she says. Blood has flowed in these past days and the talk is of vengeance. If people are speaking about the murderers in the Securitate, Ceausescu's secret police, they just say 'the terrorists'. It's a very elementary linguistic rule, which obviously helps to get over the intolerable fact that those in question lived in the neighbourhood until a matter of weeks ago, that the overwhelming majority of them where Romanians, and that they opened fire upon their own people. The designation 'terrorist' creates a distance, it creates the distance that people need in order to be able to free themselves from the nightmare of that regime. Over the years, too much of the dictatorship was seen by people as banal. Too much of that banality culminated in crime.

I abandoned Romania in 1987. I couldn't bear it any longer. I could do nothing against the crime, and I didn't want to be a silent accessory any longer. I left – and then the country was closed to me. After three years, after the bloodbath in December, for the first time I can enter it again. On the frontier at Nagylak I'm nervous, but the officials are polite. The inspection no longer acknowledges any political criteria. I'm an anonymous visitor. A fleeting glance inside my suitcase: 'What have you brought with you? Food, clothes ... all right.' I see the country's new flag, the Communist emblem is missing from it. Some of the guards are wearing armbands in the national colours. What has become of those meticulous inspections? Until just weeks ago, nothing passed without a bribe, nobody avoided harassment. It's as though quite different people now stood on the Romanian frontier, yet they're the very same. The revolution has transformed their behaviour overnight into its opposite; if you didn't know how they'd behaved up until December, you might never suspect it. This is how people turn to face the new. But what kind of guarantee can the new have, with people like that?

I'm travelling by car with friends. We're suddenly speaking faster and louder that beforehand, at the frontier. We're in the Banat, yes, where I spent the major part of my former life. When we reach the first village, there are children at the roadside, waving and shouting. What they're conveying is a mixture of victory signs and requests for chewing-gum. There are many children at the roadside, they shout and wave, they're sure of victory and confident, but they're begging. In this country the victors are destitute.

We travel through streets with gabled houses. At a certain point in the village centre, we see the results of Ceausescu's 'systematization'. The whole area bounded by four streets has been demolished: four-storey apartment blocks stand in the void, no pavement, no street, no tree between them. The apartment blocks are not ready: naked, grey concrete walls stare at the grey sky. But there are curtains at the windows, the buildings are occupied. Days later, Romanian television shows places where villages have stood, they're now snow-covered empty fields. That's in the vicinity of Lake Snagov, near Bucharest. The dictator used to have a residence there. On the way to his residence, he gradually had the villages he could see from his car demolished. The reporters stand at the

vii

roadside. Locals point out the sites to them. 'There used to be a village there', they say, pointing to empty space. The television shows the apartment blocks where the villagers now have to live. Children lie in bed, wearing caps. The flats have no heating, no water-supply. People carry water up to the flats in buckets from a surviving well. Toilets without seats stand in the open air behind the buildings, three for each block. I remember West German TV correspondent Dagobert Lindlau's report a year ago. He didn't see any of that. How many journalists over the years and decades saw nothing of the Ceausescu clan's crimes? In the end, the question always remains: how could matters get to that pass?

I spend a couple of days in the village of P., at my parents' house. The village lies close by the River Maros, at an equal distance from the cities of Arad and Temesvar. Here, on the river and at the village's edge, are the places of my childhood. Until the end of World War II, the overwhelming majority of P.'s inhabitants were German, Banat Swabians. Flight and deportation took care of half their number. Since the War, half the villagers have been Romanians. And the wave of emigration in the eighties so diminished the number of Germans that in recent times the continued existence of the German-language school has been under threat.

The revolution is present in the village of P. too. The people have chucked out the mayoress. She even smashed a portrait of Ceausescu, but it was no longer any use. Someone must have just given her a kick and told her to go to hell. The mayoress has a career behind her that is typical for the Ceausescu era. She was trained as a shoemaker, but in the nearby small town from which she comes she scarcely practised her trade. She had higher and simpler things on her mind. So she became an activist in the youth league. When the dictator peopled the offices with youngsters in order to get rid of refractory older comrades – this was at the end of the seventies – she became mayoress of P., at the age of twenty-six.

When she arrived she had nothing, people say. She swiped one of the finest houses in the village. People who emigrated had to leave their houses to the state. If one of these caught the fancy of the local authorities, they'd make sure the applicant was able to emigrate speedily, then they'd take it for themselves. That way, all parties were happy. Her house is full of furniture, real wood, all carved, people say appreciatively. They themselves haven't been able to buy real wood furniture for years; all they've had is chipboard, substitute. A substitute life. No proper bread, no proper sausage, no proper clothes.

The people are angry. They chucked out the mayoress and her deputy; the second deputy took over the official duties, till a week later they chucked him out too. They sacked the mayoress's husband who ran the cooperative society, the manager of the corn-mill, the director of the hat factory. The people dragged out the chief of the local police – or militia, as the Communists called it, consisting of three men whose main occupation was harassing or beating people and getting bribed by would-be emigrants – and gave him a thrashing. Since then he has slipped away to his home town, four villages away. The second militiaman is in prison for brutal assaults. The third is still in office under the new public order authority, now called 'police' again like before the War.

In all Romania's local authorities, a mafia of officials and administrators had formed which profited from the situation in the Ceausescu state and enriched itself unrestrainedly. The mayoress appropriated the house on the river that had belonged to the exiled Banat painter Franz Ferch. There the nomenklatura of the district used to do what was not allowed to the people: carousing and playing poker. In the village bakery, bread for the authorities – white bread – was baked separately. The populace got only black. If the mayoress needed anything, she'd send an underling to the shop. Goods were rationed, true, but if the mayoress wanted anything it would always be available from the storeroom.

Year after year the manager of the corn-mill would go off to the Bundesrepublik and make the rounds of everyone who'd emigrated from the village. He'd get them to pay up. Most of them still had relatives in Romania. Most of them wanted to be able to visit the country. Last autumn he announced a visit to me too, but I wouldn't receive him. He tried to intimidate my parents. At the end of December, the army carried out a search of the mill manager's house. They were searching for arms, there and in two other houses occupied by contacts of the Securitate.

This milling expert had no trade whatsoever. He'd been a salesman in the shop at the hat factory. His career had reached its first pinnacle when he became district secretary of the youth league. In that period he'd had himself awarded the matriculation he hadn't actually passed, by teachers ready to close both eyes. After retiring from his youth league career for reasons of age, he became first freight-controller, then manager of the mill. He maintained his position by supplying the comrades with wheat and flour and by his proven services to the Securitate – in other words, by pilfering and informing. He too owns a 'weekend house' on the river, where he used to entertain his guests.

When searches were carried out at the homes of the local nomenklatura, absurd hoards were found everywhere – of foodstuffs, drink, hi-fi equipment and stylish clothes. For decades, a mafia – legitimized via the Ceausescu family at the highest level – had infiltrated the structures of the state and instrumentalized all the institutions of society for its criminal machinations. Many if not most of these people are protesting today that they weren't really Communists at all; that they only reluctantly put up with the ideological mumbo-jumbo. Well, that's actually quite true. Communism had hardly any supporters in Romania, and none at all among such people. They weren't Communists, they were accomplices of the malefactor Ceausescu. He was their model, not as a Communist but as a criminal. They imitated him, by forever establishing new privileges for their own enjoyment and by accumulating senseless riches for which they had scarcely any use, while the nation lapsed into physical and spiritual squalor. They were parvenus who despised the culture they didn't understand and, in all they undertook, augmented nothing but bad taste. They built a caste capable of being only the parody of a social elite.

It's a cold winter. That's why all these places are so dismal, I tell myself. But I know it's not the winter. I stand on the village station. I had dirty banknotes in my hand, wafer-thin, crumpled, and for these I got a ticket, a scrap of grey paper, it says 'special ticket' on it, there aren't any real tickets, they ran out months or years ago, who still remembers, whom does it even interest?

The train arrives. It's even on time, I think, and I'm thinking like a foreigner. I am one. Three years ago I left this country, and I've long been a foreigner. I hope I don't stick out too much. I don't stick out. No more than before. I wonder about my Romanian. It hasn't deteriorated in distant lands, distance made it correct.

I sit alone in a cold railway compartment. Another twenty minutes to departure. There are footprints on the seat. 'You have to wear dark clothes to travel by train now', my mother said. A man gets in, sits down opposite me. Starts talking immediately, as is the local custom. No search for an opening, has one. 'What's the matter with the winter, where's the snow got to, what's going on with Mazilu? He's referring to Dumitru Mazilu, vice-president of the National Salvation Front which has exercised power in Romania since Ceausescu's downfall. 'He's been sacked,' the man says, 'he's under arrest. He was an officer in the Securitate. I read about it in the paper this morning.' He doesn't say in which paper. Romania has remained the country of rumours. The man says Securitate. Gives himself the cue he needs. 'Ten times as big as ours, their wages were', he says. 'We, in Arad', he says. He's one of those people who don't listen, just like to talk. In between whiles he looks out of the window, he's getting out at Hodoni, he doesn't want to miss the stop. He talks about arrests of Securitate personnel, about disarmings at which he intimates he was present. He talks about himself as though he were a revolutionary. He asks – obviously because of my accent – whether I'm from Transylvania. I tell him at once that I live in the Bundesrepublik. He asks whether there's work in the Bundesrepublik. Now that there's a new law guaranteeing all citizens freedom to travel, he – who was never allowed abroad – wants to travel at last. He wants to earn a bit of money in the Federal Republic and then come back.

People have climbed aboard, men, women. They talk loudly, stretch their legs. The train is unheated. It's cold in the compartment, as cold as in Ceausescu's day. The people talk about revelations in the media, about their own experiences under the dictatorship. They're from the countryside, they talk about the impositions. How they'd have to hand over animals they didn't even own. 'They wrote me down for ten sheep,' a woman says, 'though I haven't got any sheep at all. I said, "But I don't have any sheep." They wouldn't even listen to me', she says. They talk about travel, they want to visit relatives living in the West. The woman wants to go and see her daughter, who got married years ago and settled in Italy. Travel, an unknown terrain.

'EXISTE DUMNEZEU. TRAIASCA TOKES LASZLO', someone has written up on the façade of the Catholic church on Lahovary Square in Temesvar. 'God exists. Long live Laszlo Tokes.' The declaration is at once defiant and confident of victory. The writer looks back and looks ahead. Addresses the Communists and addresses the people. The Hungarian Reformed pastor Tokes, his conflict with both the church authorities and the Securitate, had become the trigger for the Temesvar uprising in December. The despairing people took heart from the pastor's courage; through his example, they found a strength in which they'd ceased to believe and they freed themselves. In his church Pastor Tokes, like others before him, had found support for his upright stance only at the grassroots. His church elders handed him over without shame to the Securitate, they agreed unreservedly to his deportation. Both the Reformed Church bishops responsible resigned or disappeared after the victory of the revolution. They're an eloquent illustration of how church institutions behaved under the Ceausescu regime. They too were governed by fear, mistrust, opportunism, corruption and collaboration.

So the wave of resignations and dismissals that has swept through Romanian society since the dictator's downfall had to extend also to the churches. So far only Teoctist, Patriarch of the Romanian Orthodox Church, has resigned. This largest of the country's denominations used to allow prayers for the dictator to be said in its churches; and when Ceausescu's town-planners had historic churches demolished by the dozen, its dignitaries in no single case put up any visible opposition. The other denominations behaved in a similar fashion. At the World Council of Churches, their envoys on several occasions blocked resolutions against the Ceausescu regime. Even last August, the churches were still expressing their loyalty to the Conducator (Führer) at an assembly in Bucharest. The bishop of the Evangelical Church in Transylvania, Albert Klein, also distinguished himself on that occasion. All these dignitaries ought to resign, to clear the way for a church renewal. The country finds itself in a state not least of moral disaster. The Ceausescu regime devalued everything. A return of religious ideas can be detected. People left in isolation, not just by politics, are seeking to find comfort in God. On the Opera Square in Temesvar, people stand day after day and light candles on the spots where the young people who ventured the unthinkable – that is to say, raised their voices against the criminals – were shot down in December by Ceausescu's troops. The square is now called Victory Square. Lamp-posts and walls carry the posters of an opposition party with long traditions, which was banned after the Communists took over complete power in 1948. 'Forward with God', the posters say. The central importance of God in so badly damaged a community of values places the churches under an obligation to transform themselves self-critically.

Even after the end of the Ceausescu dictatorship, there are queues everywhere, at all the shops. Even now people carry shopping-bags around with them, stand in line, wait. But they talk as well, and they're impatient. They don't want to have to wait for anything any more. Many of them still haven't really grasped the idea that the country's problems are by no means resolved with the departure of the Ceausescu clan. There are long queues at the newspaper kiosks. 'In the past, people used to read the paper in two minutes, the sports pages maybe, the classifieds; now they read everything word for word', a woman says.

The commonest word these days is probably *Libertate*, freedom. The television calls itself Free Romanian Television, lots of newspapers have the word 'Free' somewhere on their mastheads. But they're the papers from before the revolution. Formerly they were called 'Spark' or 'Red Flag'; now they're called 'Truth' and 'Rebirth'. But the same people often write in them, and they write with the same hollow enthusiasm about revolutionary events as they did in the past about decreed economic successes. In the past, if some campaign had just been announced against black-marketeers they'd write indignant reports. Now they give vent to their indignation over the luxury in the villas of the ruler's family – and they do it with blithe confidence, as though they'd never thought anything different. On television, I find the same newsreaders who were there when I went away. Then they used to praise the dictator; now they tear him to pieces. Now he has gone at last. But there's virtually no critical comment in the media on the new government. Instead, sensational journalism is the order of the day. New details are disseminated daily about the life of the hated clan. A truly free press still has to emerge. It cannot be created by the hired scribes of the bygone regime. They're not even turncoats. Years ago, one of these people said: 'We write what they ask us to.' They're probably doing the same thing again now.

Romanian politics is in a provisional state. The self-styled National Salvation Front government is legitimized only by what it does. It has defined itself as provisional and already announced free elections for April. Could be that these get deferred. Postponement is demanded above all by the opposition, which had no structures when it emerged from beneath the shadow of the dictatorship. It's just constituting itself. When Ceausescu fell, he dragged down with him the institutions of his regime, closely involved as they were in his criminal machinations. The dictatorship was over, but there were neither functioning parties nor a parliament. The Communist Party, which had almost four million members though hardly any communists, applauded the dictator as late as the last Party Congress in November. It's totally discredited and since the dictator's downfall has vanished from the country's public political life. Many of its members and parts of its apparatus have integrated themselves into the National Salvation Front; but none of them, not even prominent ones like Ion Iliescu the Front's president, openly appears as a Communist. You get the impression nobody wants to talk about this party any more. It no longer exists, leading politicians say. But it wasn't dissolved either. Who should undertake such a dissolution? It's a paradoxical situation. Angry demonstrators in Bucharest in mid-January demanded that the Party be banned. A helpless leadership of the National Salvation Front agreed to the demand and, after chaotic discussions with the demonstrators, issued a public decree banning the Communist Party – but a day later made it the subject of a referendum, and finally cancelled the referendum. This sequence of events shows the ill-defined criteria of present-day politics in Romania, just as the agonized discussion over reintroduction of the death penalty did. This discussion had arisen because the populace wanted to see the 'terrorists' hanged. Execution and vengeance are images of confusion following the downfall of a destructive dictatorship. They cannot be the beginning of a democratic future. This dilemma characterizes public life in the country. Meanwhile the Communist Party's assets have been confiscated and transferred to state ownership. Will the Party be the nation's scapegoat? It shouldn't be forgotten that society as a whole bears responsibility for the Ceausescu regime. Only the participation of all, be it only through silence, cowardice and opportunism, made possible the unbelievable crime which took place in Romania.

The party landscape now being constituted is still confused. It could hardly be otherwise. The parties appear on brief evening TV slots, presenting themselves and their programmes. They're partly reversions to political fields from the prewar period, partly new formations with general democratic and/or ecological approaches. A political development will be needed through which individual parties can define their contours. The elections will in any case come too soon for them, even if they're delayed; and if they're delayed, there's the danger of reconsolidation of the Communist power apparatus – for instance, under cover of the National Salvation Front. The latter ought to confine its tasks to the transition period up to the elections. It oughtn't to put up candidates for the parliament to be elected. Once the vote is over, it ought to consider its task done and dissolve itself, so that the country can pursue a democratic path.

The minorities in Romania have already established their own representative organizations. There's a Hungarian Union, which as a party will look after the interests of the country's largest minority, and a Democratic Forum of Romanian Germans which – because the number of Germans in Romania is so modest now – conceives of itself not as a political party but as an interest group. The future of the Romanian Germans is highly doubtful. The first issue facing them, especially since the new travel and passport laws came into force, is emigration. A large part of the minority already lives in the Federal Republic. Bounty payments and bribes ensured rapid emigration during the Ceausescu period. The dictator regarded the Romanian Germans exclusively as a commodity to be sold. Living conditions in the country had become so bad that more and more members of the German minority wanted to leave it. The cultural structures of this minority, its communities, fell into ruin long ago. There's no longer any family that isn't torn apart. For most Romanian Germans, the victory of the revolution was the signal for departure to the Bundesrepublik. In Temesvar huge queues of would-be emigrants stand in front of the passport office and the photocopying bureau. The programme adopted by the Democratic Forum of Romanian Germans is serious. Seeing that aid from the Federal Republic is also promised, it could be a real basis for a materially and spiritually secure future for the minority. But, as with many other things in this country, it's too late. Many, very many, people want to emigrate at once. Estimates vary from sixty to eighty per cent. The latter figure seems more probable. Ceausescu was overthrown ten years too late.

It's a January morning in Temesvar. I meet an acquaintance and we go into a bar. The bar's full, we look around, we're in luck, one table's still free. When the waiter notices us sitting down, he calls out to us that they've run out of beer. We nod and remain sitting. We want coffee and mineral water. The waiter comes over to the table, wipes the dirty tablecloth. 'You can get your own coffee at the snack-bar next door', he mumbles. He ignores the mineral water. We remain sitting and talking. We sit in our coats, wearing our caps. Everybody's sitting in their coats, wearing caps. The room is full of smoke and noise, you have to speak loudly in order to understand each other. After a while the waiter comes back. 'We've got some more beer,' he says in an undertone, 'Pils. If you'd like some.' We ask for a beer and a mineral water. He goes away and comes back with a beer and a mineral water. We're speaking German. When he makes out the bill, he adds up the figures in Hungarian.

On the streets, there are happy people and taciturn soldiers. Armoured cars stand in front of the army building on Freedom Square. They're bedecked with pine branches. Ribbons in the national colours are tied to them, and narrow black ribbons. It's these ribbons which recall what happened here a few weeks back. They recall the fact that all the dead still have not been found; that the atrocities perpetrated by the Securitate in December in Temesvar have still not been cleared up.

Romania is a ruined land starting out again. Democracy is incomprehensibly at hand. And the army's still on the streets, in public life, having its say. Will it some day really return to its barracks? Or will it remain a factor of Romanian politics? For the moment, there are many questions – and no answers.

Richard Wagner
January 1990

He saw carnations that looked just like carnations. He didn't buy them. He sat in cafés that looked just like cafés. We don't have any coffee today. He leafed through newspapers that looked just like newspapers. Everybody was reading page four, the sports news. He listened to opinions that sounded just like opinions. How should he respond to them? On the corner stood a man who looked just like a young man waiting. Stirner had to smile. The girl he was speaking to looked just like a pretty young girl. Perhaps she should go to the waiting young man and apologize for her lateness with a little kiss. With their arms around one another they'd walk along the boulevard and he'd present her with the carnations. Stirner gazed into the distance. He saw a dot there, which was actually not a dot at all. It was a dot in his imagination. He knew this, but clung onto it. For he lived in a country that looked just like a country. Now he could even have said the word 'paper-carnation', and it would have melted in his mouth as the word 'Cream' had melted years ago in the mouths of disc-jockeys.

Stirner saw himself as a writer. He wrote in German. Poetry, short prose pieces. It was the language of a minority. He'd published several books, but he didn't live off that. German-language books came out in small editions. He worked for a newspaper, a German-language one. As a correspondent. So he didn't have to spend every day in an editorial office. He wrote for the newspaper, and he wrote for himself, for his books. What he wrote for his books diverged more and more from what he wrote for the newspaper. He knew it. He was insecure. He could foresee that he'd soon be helpless. He'd lived in this city for several years now. With Sabine. Sabine worked as a German teacher. She taught German as a foreign language. She had no fixed job. Year after year, just supply classes. First in one school, then in another. German lessons were regarded as a subsidiary subject; they were something which could even be dispensed with. If too many school days were missed. Because the pupils had been sent for too long to the fields. In autumn, on account of the harvest.

A colleague had come. On account of the newspaper's sales. They travelled to villages, they visited schools. Everywhere the same thing. Begging. To get rid of subs. For a publication which didn't interest anyone. Showing their credentials: Party press. Already a semi-threat. Some people let themselves be impressed, others made no attempt to hide their annoyance, many even their contempt. They didn't talk a lot on the way. Just as much as was necessary. They had no common concerns. The paper they were selling didn't interest the colleague. Stirner had noticed this straight off. The colleague simply worked there. And Stirner had by now grown accustomed to people of this kind. They drew their salary, and wrote as much as they had to. No more, no less. Over the years piece payments had been reduced to a minimum, all that by now mattered was to justify one's salary. People of this kind were more and more frequently to be met with in editorial offices. And if they could write even a bit, they were highly popular with editors-in-chief. They wrote every kind of trash, you see, and were entirely without scruple. Composing a leading article: for them it was like putting out the garbage pail. They washed their hands and that was the end of it.

The colleague who was travelling with Stirner was a kind of jack-of-all-trades in the editorial office. Every editorial office has one. To be more accurate: every editor-in-chief. For the colleague was also available for all kinds of private assignments. Chauffeuring the editor-in-chief, ever since the latter's official car had been removed; getting rid of people on the telephone; keeping his ears open for whatever his colleagues might be saying; always present, well-informed, on hand, useful.

So they'd travel along and launch into their patter. Those little forms of blackmail. As you appreciate, we're a German paper after all ... it's important for our community that we continue to appear ... we write about the cultural life of our German community ... we've already written even about your own home town, after all, about your schools and how many German classes you've still actually got ... German teachers, and pupils too of course, can contribute to our newspaper, we're delighted at every letter ... we've even got a pupils' page, short letters about school events, extra-curricular activities, outings, class parties, the pupil's name gets printed, of course ... here are a few diaries too, with our paper's imprint, you can dole them out to the pupils ... the sub prices are given inside, for three months, six months and twelve months ... the best thing, of course, would be subs for twelve months, or for six.

They boarded the train that went to the next little place, and the seats opposite them were empty. A young woman sat down and started talking at once. Stirner had known her at high school, she'd matriculated a year before him. Her voice was familiar to him. Her way of talking too. She'd spent five years at Piatra Neamţ in Moldavia, allocated there, she said, and might never have got away again. Now she was back at home, she said, she'd spent half the autumn in the School Inspectorate waiting rooms, well you know them, totally corrupt, didn't want to give her a post at any price, and she with the kid, on her own she stressed, but Stirner didn't ask her what then had become of her husband ... she, with the kid, forever on the stairs, and Comrade Inspector and the rest they're never available, never have time for you, constantly invent meetings, but she'd simply not let herself be fobbed off, so they'd chucked her this job at a nursery school, so there you have it, that's what she'd studied philology for, for this supply job. Now she had to travel every morning and back again in the afternoon, with some luck the train's not running late, she has to run from the station, if she isn't on time the headmistress, a real hellcat, knocks off her first hour, and at home the kid's waiting, and then there's still the shopping, she said, the shopping, if there's anything to be had anyway, what on earth am I supposed to give the kid when there isn't anything, and who knows how next year will be?

4

The train stopped. We're already in the vineyards, she said. Seems to be going smoothly today.

On another occasion Stirner was waiting for the bus with the colleague in the centre of a village. And since they had to talk, they talked. And since the colleague knew that Stirner published books, he suddenly asked – it was quiet, it was still early, they'd got through quickly at the school, and the postmaster had told them, sure, about the subs, if it went on like this in the village with the emigration they'd soon have to bring out a newspaper in Urdu, which was intended as an allusion to the number of Gypsies in the locality – well, the colleague suddenly asked: Do you know the poet U? The poet U was a Romanian poet. Yes, said Stirner, he knew the poet U. They'd been students together at Jassy, the colleague said. A very clever lad. Even then. Had to work for his living all the time he was writing his dissertation. He didn't come back from the West though, a few years ago, said Stirner. A clever lad, murmured the colleague, gazing towards the end of the street. That was where the bus would come from.

Again they left a school where once again every kind of promise had been made to them, and the colleague said: Now we're going on to T's. T had been a correspondent for the newspaper. A few months before he'd vanished. At some point he'd called up and said: Take me off the masthead, I'm in Munich. How he'd got there, nobody knew. There were only rumours: he'd left by car, his wife too, fake passports, bribery, the usual stories. I know where his house is, the colleague said. We're going there. Ask a few questions. Someone must be there, after all. What are we supposed to ask, then? Stirner inquired. Oh, how he got away. And what he's doing there. The boss is dying to know.

The colleague's features wore a thin smile. It was an open secret that the correspondent had been a pal of the editor-in-chief's. He used to supply the latter with vegetables, drive him round on his trips, invite him to his home. T didn't write

5

a line for the paper. People said he deposited his entire salary into his bank account. It was to be presumed that T simply used the job as a cover, so that he could pursue other affairs. What kind of affairs these were, was unclear. The hypotheses moved on the level of wild rumours.

At all events, his parents were market gardeners – in these times a lucrative occupation. The colleague and Stirner stopped in front of a showy Swabian house, a high fence blocked off the courtyard from their view. They rang. At once a dog began to bark. They rang again. The street was empty, house upon house, each one a little fortress. No one was to be seen. The dog behind the fence was barking like mad. Suddenly they heard a woman's voice shouting something to the dog. The dog went on barking. The woman's voice kept on at the dog. Then the gate opened. Before them stood an old woman in Swabian costume. A dark headscarf almost concealed her face. Her eyes were mistrustful. We're colleagues of your grandson's, the colleague said. Her face grew stony. She stared at her hand. But he's not here any more. That's what we'd like to talk about, said the colleague. There's nobody here, she repeated. Not even my children. I can hardly manage to tie the dog up, she went on. I don't know about anything. We just want to talk a bit, the colleague said. You'd better come in then, she said hesitantly.

They entered the house. The colleague allowed his gaze to roam, as though he might be able to discover somewhere in this house a clue to T's flight. The old woman conducted them to a room furnished with contemporary junk. In recent years, most people had got rid of their old Swabian furniture and were keeping up with the times. I don't know anything, said the old woman. He's gone. I'll never see him again. She fell silent. What were we working for? She fell silent. The young people leave. She fell silent. The young people have to leave. We old ones stay behind. She wept. Then we old ones have to leave too. She wept. We're too small to change anything.

Let's go, said Stirner.

In the station, the colleague saw a discarded ticket lying on the platform. He picked it up, examined it thoroughly, read the destination and date, tucked it away. You can get a refund, he said.

S tirner lay on the divan and read. The divan came from Sabine's grandmother. It had stood in the hallway, in the long cool house. Stirner put his book down beside him on the chair. He thought about the people who'd sat upon the divan, in the twenties. He couldn't picture them, though he knew quite a lot about their way of life. He pricked up his ears. He had the impression he'd heard the clink of bottles, as though beer were being unloaded. He stood up, went into the other room and looked out of the window, over the back of the grocery shop below. That was where the goods were unloaded. When a delivery van drove up – ordinary trucks, or in recent times even tractors with trailers – people gathered at once. You'd hear shouts, see women at windows, see women running. In the twinkling of an eye a queue would form, for if it were not actually raining or snowing most goods would be sold on the street behind the shop, through a little window in the wall: frozen chickens, cheese, canned stuff, instant coffee (even this sometimes came), Hungarian margarine. People would stand four abreast in a long queue on the street, holding their identity documents in their hands: chickens, for instance, could be had only on production of a city residence document. Loud voices would penetrate up to the fifth floor. People would be quarrelling. Somebody would have pushed in front.

Stirner had long understood the need to avoid certain themes. There were themes that were compromised, ideologically appropriated, finished. Nothing to be done with them. No sooner would readers see the headline than all would be clear to them. They'd read no further. They'd be nauseated. Most people had stopped reading between the lines. What was the point. Many people subscribed simply for wrapping paper, and in the country for toilet paper. Cut into rectangles the newspaper sheets would hang in the earth closet, most would have pictures of the President and his wife. The papers were full of these. Once Stirner had written a profile of a woman painter, and when the text appeared – it was two weeks before some Party conference – he found a sentence in it saying that the artist was creating with special enthusiasm under the banner of the forthcoming Party resolutions. The profile bore Stirner's signature, this one sentence had been written by the editor-in-chief. Stirner had protested, there was some tiny hope that next time they wouldn't proceed so brazenly. But the basic trouble was that hardly anyone in the editorial office understood what he was on about. In the eyes of his colleagues, this was all just nit-picking and hair-splitting. What after all did a sentence of that kind matter, one more or less? Why was it so important to him anyway? All he wanted was to work less for the paper, draw his salary, and have time for his books, wasn't that so? But these poets were notorious. Took shelter behind moralistic notions. As though people didn't know. Stirner had seen his job with the newspaper as the only possibility of being able to carry on in this country. The editors too probably thought they could get along with this admittedly rather complicated individual. Besides, they'd made a practice of having an *enfant terrible* around. It looked good to the public, and the editor-in-chief could say he was protecting awkward people.

T he President had already been announced days ago. The street scene was full of groups from the city cleansing department, toiling zealously away. Lorries laden with flags and slogans drove through the streets. Workmen stood on crane-trucks and fixed flagpoles to the lampposts on the main streets, especially on the Corso between the Opera House and the Orthodox Cathedral. It was from the balcony of the Opera that the President, on what the media termed his working visits, used to deliver his speeches to the population assembled on Opera Square. On the eve of the occasion, a colossal portrait of the President would be mounted on the front of the Opera House. It was the same badly-drawn image that hung throughout the land. He appeared much younger in it than he actually was. To the left and right of the balcony, flags would be unfurled: the red-yellow-and-blue of the national flag, with its coat-of-arms; and the red of the Party flag, hammer-and-sickle in the corner. On the buildings that stand diagonally across from the Opera balcony, four-storey residences from the twenties, topical slogans would be hung from mobile cranes: entire windowed façades would be covered with letters. In the rooms behind, it was said, agents from the Securitate always sit during the President's speeches. From the Opera balcony, you could look directly across to the Orthodox Cathedral. But since it was notorious that the President couldn't abide to see a church, pneumatic cranes used to hoist slogan-covered hoardings so high in the air that the view of the Cathedral from the balcony would be crudely blocked off. Here on the square the masses will stand tomorrow. They'll be brought in from the factories in columns. Above their heads they'll hold slogans, flags, and pictures of the President and his wife. Hours before the event – the Grand Popular Assembly as it was called in the official terminology – they'll be brought here. They'll wait for the President, and the square will be cordoned off so that everyone has to stay there, and if anyone should nevertheless leave, then a day

10

will be deducted from his month's wages, thought Stirner as he walked across the paved surface where the pigeons still hopped and pecked at the bread passers-by threw them, pensioners and children.

He walked past the fountain, which played only on the National Holiday, in August. Then children would sit on the parapet and hold their hands in the unfamiliar jet of water spurting from the ancient fish's mouth.

Early in the morning Stirner boarded a silent train. People were whispering. Some were sleeping. He held the local tabloid paper in the meagre light coming from outside, and read meaningless items like a person thirsty for information. The train left, he didn't keep track of how often it stopped. At a city station he got out. The city lay behind the station, nothing of it visible. Another train stopped in a siding and he climbed aboard. It was raining. Few people were sitting on the benches. They had country faces and talked about the need for rain and the height of the wheat. The train travelled through damp fields. Everything was very green. He got out at a station. Behind it high trees stood. If you looked carefully, you could make out flat roofs among the trees. He asked for the coach depot. The bus was packed. It travelled along an asphalted road, it stopped in villages whose names Stirner forgot again. The region was hilly. When Stirner dismounted, the rain had ceased. Dark clouds tossed above the woods. He stood by the side of the road. He saw damp houses. He went over to them. The Centre must be somewhere. He found a little building upon which a red glass sign was fixed. He went in. Behind a door that looked like the door of a living-room he came across a man. Stirner said he was a journalist. The man proffered his hand. It was the Party Secretary. Stirner said he was looking for the playwright who wrote the amateur theatricals. You've arrived too late then, said the Party Secretary, the playwright's dying. He doesn't know any longer who or where he is. Sometimes he runs out of the house screaming, wrapped in a white sheet. He used to arrange beautiful cultural programmes for us. On holidays. You can't talk to him any more, but if you'd like to speak to his son just go over to the factory. In the bus Stirner got another seat. It was raining. The landscape was flat again.

Through the window Stirner saw a young woman walk over to the refuse bin. She was wearing old clothes. The clothes didn't match. She climbed onto a bucket full of rubbish and peered into the bin. With her left hand she clutched the edge of the bin, with her right she poked around inside the bin, every now and then throwing a piece of mouldy bread onto the grass. A mufflered child stood there, collecting the pieces of bread in a light-blue plastic bag.

S tirner had been to the country and, for the first time in a long while, he'd spoken the dialect of his childhood with his parents. When he was back in the city again, he had a conversation and dialect expressions kept slipping into his sentences.

When he came to the city, the editor-in-chief used to stay in the Party hotel. The Party hotel was a small building in a quiet street, behind a park. The street was in the big shots' neighbourhood. Little traffic, two-storey villas with garden and garage. You'd rarely see anyone in the courtyards. Here and there, elderly men enigmatically mute. In front of the villas, parked cars with low numbers. Sometimes you'd see a chauffeur lifting heavy parcels from the luggage-boot and carrying them into the house. Formerly the bourgeoisie had lived here. The Party hotel had no business plate to indicate that it was a hotel. You went in through an ordinary double door and at once found the reception desk in front of you. You had to go past it if you wanted to get to the canteen, the buffet, or your room. At the buffet, the people from the houses on the quiet streets of the neighbourhood would do their shopping. Food that you couldn't find in the city. In the canteen, you could eat cheaply or else take food away. Stirner knew all this by hearsay. He climbed the stairs behind the editor-in-chief. The editor-in-chief occupied a suite. Even a desk stood in one of the rooms. He gestured to Stirner to take a seat. His face remained expressionless. He looked very busy, but his gestures gave nothing away. He sat down behind the desk. Yes, what Stirner wrote was good, of course, he said suddenly. Now Stirner knew that he was up to something. With this sentence he'd given himself away. Behind this sentence, a single carefully constructed edifice lay concealed. Stirner resolved to be on his guard. No doubt about that, the editor-in-chief went on. But so far as our nationality is concerned, it's always necessary to bear all the factors in mind. Stirner decided not to understand. He nodded uncertainly. Everything that goes to make up the concept of community, the editor-in-chief added. He made a little pause. Then suddenly said in a loud voice: That's where newspaper reports can be very important. People's work. We must show how the work is theirs. How they enjoy the

15

fruits of their work. The editor-in-chief glanced briefly at Stirner. Everything you write, he said, must produce that effect. He leaned forward slightly. His voice grew lower. Now he's emphasizing his complicity, thought Stirner. We must show what's positive, the achievements. We're an organ of the Party, that has to be said straight off, doesn't it? And our task is to acquaint readers with the Party's directives. He shifted on his chair. Of course, not in the form of crude slogans. No. He sat up straight, and a smile came into his face, as though he'd had a brainwave. The reader must swallow the pill. He made a gesture as though to convey a pill to his mouth. Pursed his lips. Paused. They mustn't notice anything until they've swallowed the pill. Then it's too late. That's how you must write, the editor-in-chief concluded. He stood up. You can even publish the reports as a book afterwards, he said – and was already standing in front of Stirner with outstretched hand. Stirner went down the stairs alone. From the canteen there emerged a little old man, wiry, freshly shaven, in a suit, dishes in his hand. Stirner let him go ahead. Even a veteran of the Underground like that, he thought, his ideals reduced to a meal ticket. Survives the Underground, survives Stalin, survives the Thaw, now the President feeds him.

S tirner too knew those sympathetic informers, the kind who has a ready ear for your worries. You don't have the impression he's pumping you. It's the nice colleague at work, the former schoolmate, whom you sometimes bump into in the street. Let's go and have a beer. He listens to you sympathetically. He understands you. Even in political matters he shares your opinions, in confidence. He just expresses himself more sparingly. And lets you talk. He's even reluctant about doing it. But there were all those ugly stories at the time, after all. He shakes his head in disbelief. And since then, They come round. What am I supposed to do? I don't tell them anything in particular. What they already know anyhow. He has a mischievous little smile on his face. Sometimes I simply have to. They're on the fifth beer. Why do you have to shoot your mouth off, anyway? Like last week in the bar. Understand me. He puts his hand on your arm, and doesn't remove it till you pull your arm away. You'd think they were really suffering. They were quite capable of explaining how they're the victims, not you. And you're even supposed to help them do their job, on top of everything. If they've once wormed themselves in. They'd be quite capable of telling you it could just as easily have happened to you. So come along now, give us a few nice little items on yourself.

Such fellows couldn't do anything more to Stirner. If they came to the table, he'd just carry on with his usual speech against the regime, crude and direct, albeit without details. If anyone tried discreetly to catch his attention, he'd wave him aside. I've already said it all long ago anyway, he'd usually say then. It had the ring of a pat phrase, whose meaning wasn't quite clear to himself. He'd think no more about it.

In any case, the informers would show no particular interest in his speeches. They'd seem more bored than anything. Obviously, none of them wanted to hear definitions of the regime; after a while, they'd usually go away. Had another appointment. Right after. Worse luck.

17

There were days when nothing at all would occur to him. He could virtually feel the dullness in his head. On such days, he was incapable of writing anything. He ascribed this situation to the general void. His surroundings had a paralysing effect upon him. He saw before him a succession of such days; he saw them grow ever more frequent; he saw himself thinking less and less, more and more schematically. He'd not write anything else. Nothing.

Stirner and Sabine had gone off into the countryside. They walked along the edge of an acacia wood. It was a Sunday morning in April, with sunshine in whose warmth you'd sometimes shiver. They walked along a narrow, well-trodden path, now one behind the other, now side by side; when they encountered bicycles they'd halt. The bicycles were ridden by mufflered men with expressionless faces, on their luggage-carriers they had bags from which grass poked. In the distance you could hear dogs barking. Stirner had already picked up a stick lying by the wayside. Sabine talked. She was forever seeing something new in the landscape, something that Stirner didn't see, and she'd point it out to him. Then he'd see it too, but alone and of his own accord he wouldn't have seen it. Perhaps it was also true that his interest contained a hint of pretence. At least that's how it seemed to him, and he caught himself wanting to have his own little say, and the impression of pretence grew still stronger. Stirner's thoughts were elsewhere, or it was just that the landscape brought back his childhood. He looked at the tops of the trees, he saw the cawing crows rise from their nests and felt as though his gaze were skimming the contours of another time. They arrived at a weathered stone bridge and gazed for a while at the babble of the watercourse below. I once fell through the ice here, said Stirner suddenly, one January it was. I walked half the day with wet shoes and didn't go home till evening.

S ometimes he felt an aversion to the Romanian language. He'd catch himself making some disparaging comment. It was a matter of conceptual poverty. Or he'd laugh at a verse that came over as flowery. He knew that this was an aversion to the State language. It was his way of snubbing the State language, a language in which he was confronted by slogans, empty phrases, big lies. It was like the aversion to Russian in his childhood. The aversion that made him incapable of learning the Cyrillic alphabet. He still hadn't mastered it to this day, which he found very annoying. Russian at that time meant the Russians. And the Russians had come. This grown-up phrase was deeply embedded among his first words. Russian meant the Russians, Romanian the State. He'd never be able to write in Romanian. This was clear to him, however reluctant he was to admit it. One spends a lifetime shaking off the assumptions of a lifetime.

When Sabine was still working at that engineering enterprise, she was approached one day by a tall, blond, broad-shouldered man with watery blue eyes. He sat alone with her in the office, and launched into a discussion. So you're working here as a translator. We haven't got to know one another yet. There are matters of security here. You do interpreting too. We often get foreigners coming here. After all, it's an important enterprise. To put it simply: the reports on discussions with these people are meaningless. This file here – he rapped on a file lying in front of him which contained the reports the engineers had to write after their foreign business partners had left – this file here, he repeated, is totally useless. We need concrete stuff. Every man has a weakness, after all. Lots drink, others chase women. Anyhow, you know the ropes. Perhaps you could ... and besides, oh yes, write this, he slid a sheet of paper across to her and began to dictate: I herewith pledge myself. I'm not writing that, said Sabine. I'm not signing that. And anyway, what you want from me doesn't come under my conditions of service. The man reached for the paper, screwed it up and threw the ball into her face. It fell to the ground. Sabine remained sitting. The man stood up, retrieved the ball of paper, opened his briefcase, threw it in and closed the case. Before going, he told Sabine: You'll be sorry for this. A month later the manager summoned her and informed her that the enterprise no longer had any employment for her, they no longer needed translators, the engineers understood German anyway. The form of dismissal was not entirely legal, but it was also not entirely illegal, like most things in this country. At all events, since then Sabine had landed only temporary supply jobs, in teaching.

My wife got a negative decision too, said the deputy chief editor during the break in the meeting. He was the Number Two on the editorial staff, the educated individual who ran the whole show. He made the paper readable. The boss never even read the newspaper, he'd once told Stirner.

They were sitting in a bar, Stirner, the Number Two, and another staff editor from the cultural pages who enjoyed the latter's confidence. The Number Two had summoned a waiter, a German, and – in a faintly conspiratorial tone – engaged him in a brief discussion, as a result of which they secured a table farther back, ate trout and drank white wine.

Then along He comes to the meeting and judges material about which he knows nothing, even gives us advice, you've heard it yourself, said the Number Two. But what are we supposed to do, we need him. So long as he's got his Party position, the newspaper's safe.

It was a favourite theme among the German-speaking journalists, speculating about how long it would last, keep going, as they put it, and which of the German-language papers would hold out longest, be left, as they put it. For it was clear to them all that after a while it would go. The older ones had made their calculation, it'll be there till we retire, then we'll go as well. Namely to the Bundesrepublik.

He didn't do a thing for my wife, said the Number Two, even though he's on the passport committee. But don't take it so hard, he told Stirner. He came within an ace of saying: We're all in the same boat. At any rate, it's a good thing you told us at once about those fellows coming that time. Well, you know that as long as you're working for us, you don't necessarily need to talk to them. As I've told you, if they show up again, which I don't suppose they will, just let me know. And refer to the fact that you're answerable to your boss. They should come and see the boss. He laughed unrestrainedly, revealing a row of false teeth. They looked as if they were actually a bit too big. Of course, we'd have to be in the know too. For example, if you talk to foreigners, write me a note, any old thing, and I'll put it in the drawer. That's important, if they come. Then they can't say a thing. And you may as well know, in such cases the boss will back you up.

He looked at the other editor, who until then had been listening politely. It was a subordinate kind of listening, with sips and nods. He'd dissected the trout expertly. In his gestures you could discern the bourgeois home in which he'd grown up. The times had changed, the family had lost everything, as people used to say in such cases, but he'd retained the manners: even as an editor on the Party newspaper, he wrote the finer things on the cultural pages – the dessert after the propaganda stew.

He told us straight off too, said the Number Two. And that's the best way.

They ordered another bottle of white wine. The waiter approached with a little bow as though he wanted to ask how his guests were doing, but he didn't ask anything. The mute intimation was evidently sufficient. It was the last bottle they ordered, since in such company you didn't go on the booze.

But we've got people in the office who don't breathe a word, said the Number Two. That's the problem.

He looked briefly at the other editor, and the latter smiled knowingly. Stirner asked nothing, he knew a question now would have been out of place. If they wanted to say anything more, they'd say it anyhow; if not, a question simply aroused mistrust. They drank.

Our colleague Z's wife wasn't allowed to travel either, said the Number Two. Though it was absolutely necessary for her to travel to the West. Because of her cancer. Stirner said nothing. I'll give you a piece of advice, said the Number Two. Have a try with the boss. Invite him home – he made a little pause, designed to underline all the significance that was latent in the little sentence – perhaps he'll have a word with that lot, he added quickly. It'd be a chance. They

23

drank. Colleague, said the Number Two, I'll tell you a story. And he began to talk ramblingly about an Austro-Hungarian Imperial officer, about his wives and children who were buffeted by every turn of the wind, a story which extended over several decades and ended with the fact that the Imperial officer was a relative of the Number Two's. Isn't that just like a novel? Tell me.

As Stirner sat in the train again he thought: Lucky I'm just a correspondent. Day after day in that office, it'd be unbearable. And every so often in the canteen of the local paper too, people used to say: You're nicely off! They can't rope you in for every damned thing. You're just not here. Things were bad again today. The boss arrived from the Party committee, around ten or so, and threw a fit. They'd probably hauled him over the coals again. Yet again, not enough Party policy in the paper. What they'd like best would be to fill the papers up entirely with reports. Industry, agriculture, achievements. *Basta*. What on earth are people supposed to read? The circulation's gone down again. Those were the conversations at the canteen table, unless there was something to buy. For in that case most people would be busy queuing. From twelve on, the editorial offices would begin to empty. A rumour would sweep from floor to floor. There are chickens today. Hastily they'd hand in the stuff they'd composed, fulfilment of the plan at B, determination, expression of joy, gratitude, beloved Leader, that's the way the words would bubble out of the typewriters, chickens, two per person, and lemons, and salami, a kilo, or some of that sausage, you know the smoked one for ninety Lei, and butter, I never reached the butter, it ran out before I got there. But the best gets dished out at the back. Tell me, did you ever see the boss queuing? Or his wife?

S abine arrived back from school. German as a foreign language. What lessons! Before even the word 'apple' had been learnt, you'd already have such items of vocabulary as 'agricultural-production-cooperative' and 'over-fulfilment-of-the-plan'. You were meant to teach that. Sabine skipped a number of lessons, she left out the patriotic poems. She wrote words like 'salt' and 'apricot' and 'duck' on the blackboard. Her colleague, the school's other German teacher, went to the Principal and reported her. Sabine wasn't sticking to the textbook. In the breaks, the teachers would sit in the staffroom. The men would tell risqué jokes, the women would laugh pointedly. Sabine would sit on a bench in the yard and smoke. You shouldn't smoke in front of the pupils. You should smoke in the room set aside for that purpose. And you should speak in the room set aside for that purpose. In the conference hall. Twice a week. The latest initiatives of our President. In our field, of course. And in other fields of work. Bringing the achievements home to the pupils. Nothing falls outside patriotic education. Not even mathematics. Give some thought to the exercises. In English lessons, no map of Britain must hang on the wall, but a Romanian one. It should be clear to them all by now. The Principal's speaking. He loves making long speeches. There's chattering in the back rows. So he's got something wrong with his prostate. Who? The one in the picture on the wall over there. Oh, I thought you meant the Comrade Principal. Tittering. A little quiet back there, please, comrades! You ladies can ask to speak later on. Our topic for today. Sabine had been through that once, it had been enough for her. The Principal was threatening. She walked past him, she looked right through him. Why don't you come in a skirt? Teachers are supposed to appear before the pupils in skirts, not in trousers like that. You should come in a skirt. Sabine went to her class. A pupil stood up and asked: Comrade Teacher, why have we skipped this poem?

A decade ago, after the last floods, Stirner had for the first
time been in the house that had belonged to his great-
grandfather. The waters had already retreated from the
meadow. The damp clay lay everywhere. Stirner had been
there with his father. They walked through the building. For
many years it had belonged to other people, strangers had
lived there – that's what everyone used to say. That's where
your great-grandparents' bedroom was, said his father.
They walked through the rooms. They walked over the
clayey ground. A clayey smell hung in the air. The sun shone
through the roof, the bare wattles jutted from the walls. They
built that way because of the floods, his father said. Posts,
and in between wattles. Over that, clay; and on top of the
clay, lime. When the waters came, they used to put the
furniture into the loft. And the waters would come, wild and
gurgling, and wash away the clay. The wattles would
remain, the waters would retreat. Today there's no longer
anything to be seen of the house. Weekend houses stand in its
place. Three or four. Cassette-players blare in the yard. The
men put the roast on the grill, the women bake potatoes.
Behind the little houses stand the cars. They have low
numbers.

On the dial he turned to short-wave. It was late morning, after ten at any rate. He came across noises and traces of voices. No, that wasn't speech. Those weren't words. A few bars of music and a long whistling sound which interfered with everything. He stopped at the whistling sound, but the whistling sound disappeared. He'd owned this radio for ten years. It no longer worked properly, but you could still hear things. A Romanian piece of equipment. There weren't any like that in the shops now. Now there were no more short-waves at all. He tried again, held his finger on the aerial. It had come loose. He'd wedged in a paper pellet. He turned the knob more carefully. He thought he'd just got hold of a station. The radio stood on the windowsill. That way the reception was better. Though at this hour, what was there to listen to. The radio worked on batteries. R 20, the commonest kind. You could usually get them. When the power failed, he could at least listen to the radio. He gave up. He switched to medium-wave. To the morning opera.

VERSO

6 Meard Street
London W1V 3HR

Telephone
01-437 3546
01-434 1704

REVIEW COPY

EXIT
A Romanian Story

By Richard Wagner

Translated by Quintin Hoare

£6.95 paperback
ISBN 0 86091 510 7

£24.95 hardback
ISBN 0 86091 243 4

Publication Date: 21st June 1990

For further information about the publication
of this title please contact the Verso publicity department
at the above address.
We would be grateful to receive copies
of all reviews published.

Stirner had to find out for himself that he couldn't stick it out in a system like this. Everyone had to find this out for themselves. In a regime that occupies the language, you can't express opinions. If you wanted to write realistic literature and said so, you'd find yourself already on the regime's home ground. For the regime too called for a realistic literature. And it was the regime that decided what was realistic. What you yourself regarded as realistic was then seen as unrealistic, it was hostile to the State or anti-socialist. Words were two-faced. The regime wanted a critical literature: 'The residues of the past have to be criticized.' It wanted a committed literature: 'In certain spheres, defects still áppear.' It wanted a courageous literature: 'Even under socialism there are contradictions.' The regime always meant an affirmative literature: 'What we need is constructive criticism.' Words had long ago been expropriated. Clowns cavorted on the regime's open stage and were prodigal with words.

He dreamed he was in Bucharest. He had a reading. The reading was to take place in a labyrinthine building. He couldn't find the hall. He lost his luggage. He climbed higher and higher inside the building. Suddenly he had the impression of stepping into the open air. It was a cemetery. A naked couple was tussling in an open grave. When they saw him, they pulled a bedcover over themselves. They were laughing. On another grave he discovered part of his luggage. He wanted to get it, but he couldn't stir from the spot. All was silent. Far below you could hear a muffled sound like the distant roar of traffic. As though this were a roof garden. On a skyscraper. After a long while he reached the grave upon which his luggage lay. His manuscripts were missing. All the bags, and there were more than he'd ever owned, contained clothes. Clothes of which he had no memory. He dragged himself to the cemetery wall. He looked down from the skyscraper. He could see into a hall. The hall was full of people. You could hear a babble and hum of voices, somewhat muted, like before the beginning of a performance. Stirner moved around among the people, no one took any notice of him. He thought he could see only familiar faces, but he couldn't have said whose faces they were. Everywhere there were exits. You could hardly take two steps without finding yourself at an exit. Stirner tried it a couple of times. It was always the same. He was afraid of losing the room. He stood still. At once he found himself in the middle of the room. He took a step, a single step, and already he was at an exit. He decided to stand still. Then he noticed that nobody was moving. They were all just talking. Stirner too began to talk. But no one answered him. Then he noticed that those present weren't talking to each other, but to themselves. Moreover, you couldn't understand what they were saying, and if you tried to move a step nearer you'd once again be standing at an exit. You could just hear this steady, muted clamour of words. Stirner talked, and realized that he didn't himself understand what he was saying. But he could now see the contours of the vault in which they found themselves, the more he spoke the more distinct its outlines became. The vault must be located somewhere beneath the cemetery, he thought. It was just the shadow of a thought. It quickly faded. The sound of words continued undisturbed.

The Writers' Institute stood on the boulevard, an expropriated villa in a courtyard behind a wrought-iron railing. In the courtyard, to the left of the gate, there was a protected tree. The writers have got a protected tree, people would say with a laugh. They should put a conservation order on the whole lot. Years ago, it had been at night, closing time, two writers, friends of Stirner's, had come to blows under this tree. He was always reminded of it whenever he saw the tree. The affair had never been explained, 'rowdies' people would say, they didn't like to talk about it, one of the combatants was supposedly the cousin of a Securitate officer, but that was just a rumour, the matter was best forgotten. The main entrance to the building was used for access to the Union's executive offices. These were situated on the first floor. There were always writers sitting around on the plush chairs in the corridors, waiting for a Union president – who remained invisible – in order to lay before him their concerns: money, prizes, foreign trips, accommodation, jobs.

On the ground floor, in the rear part of the building, was the writers' restaurant, which was officially registered as a canteen. It could be approached from the courtyard by way of a narrow side-entrance. You reached the dining-room through the kitchen lobby. Inside it was quite dark, the panelled walls gave the room a gloomy air. At canteen tables, with white tablecloths that contrasted with the panelling, the writers sat chair to chair. At a glance you could see that this room had once had some other function. It looked as though it were under occupation. The entire building might give you this impression, as though following an insurrection it had provisionally been converted into a command centre.

Stirner gazed questingly about him. The head waiter was already coming over, in a dark, greasy suit, with black-framed spectacles adorning his broad face. How can I help you? he asked. This meant: What are you doing here? Or more precisely: No admittance. Only writers are allowed in here. I'm with the Germans over there, said Stirner, pointing to a table in the corner at which he'd caught sight of his friends. The waiter cast a fleeting glance in the direction in which Stirner had pointed, nodded as though he now knew all about it, made a little bow and a gesture of welcome. Stirner was a customer. Consequently a writer. What the hell. He made his way to his friends' table, in the meantime they'd organized an empty chair.

Here the writers were on their own, just as elsewhere the journalists were on their own, and elsewhere the architects and the civil engineers and the construction workers and the agricultural workers and the football players and the army officers. All wished to be on their own, to eat cheaply and to talk about their interests undisturbed. Like in a private box. The whole country seemed to Stirner to consist of such private boxes. No one looked at anyone else. They all kept their eyes on the stage. And all saw the same rubbishy old performance. But they couldn't tell one another. They were sitting in private boxes, each conscious of his significance, and from box to box like waiters went the people from the Securitate.

The writers were talking about literature. However did that Márquez win the Nobel Prize, a Romanian lyric poet was saying. He'd published two slim volumes, without compromising so people claimed, was seen as a hot tip. He had cirrhosis, but went on drinking. Well, what's Márquez written, he asked. He hasn't written anything. From a bottle he poured himself vodka into a tumbler. Who should have won it then, asked Stirner. Who, said the poet, why Borges of course, there's a writer, not this fellow ...

Stirner had no desire to ask more. It was just the usual invective all over again. All leftists are communists, the communists brought the Russians, the Russians ruined the country, and the leftists can't write, they're just deadbeat writers, social commitment, tommyrot, what room's left for

33

aesthetics, it's nothing but proletkultism, propaganda. Stirner had heard it all enough times, he turned away. Antonescu should have halted on the Dniester, a Romanian writer was saying very loudly at the other end of the table.

At two tables pulled together the up-and-coming authors were sitting and singing. One was playing a guitar. Setting poems to music, 'folk' they called it. They were celebrating as a victory the appearance of an anthology. The anthology had been gathering dust at the publishers' for five years, what had appeared was roughly half of the originally chosen texts. With the anthology they'd entered into general contention, now they were authorized to publish books. That was the sequence: first in an anthology, then your debut. Now they were in the running. They could be off. Who'll produce more books, who'll win more prizes. Who'll get the first trip abroad, who'll secure a Union post. Material for a life.

A woman was going from table to table saying: Would you believe it, I don't know who they are? And then: Do you have any money? They want me to keep my trap shut. Nobody asked what she meant. Occasionally someone would give her a ten-Lei coin, for a vodka as they'd put it. Why ever did you Germans lose the war, a critic asked and called for a vodka. And what if you'd won it? You behave as though you'd won it.

The waitress brought a new round.

Three times my volume went before the Cultural Commission, said an elderly lyric poetess. She had on a broad, black hat, her lips were painted scarlet. Each time they wanted new changes. Until I'd had enough. I told the editor, do what you want. The book already gives me the creeps.

She sipped at her glass. A young woman author had come in. She looked sadly at the company and said, more to herself than anything: They won't let me travel again.

Though all chairs in the room were occupied and several

34

people were vainly keeping an eye open for an empty place, one table in the left-hand corner remained inviolate. The chairs had been propped with their backs against the table, as a sign that it was taken. Nobody asked about this table. An old writer usually sat there, alone or with his young lady friend, with his dog and sometimes with his guests. As a rule he sat there in silence and watched the goings-on. Occasionally he'd beckon someone over to his table. This was regarded as an honour. In his youth he'd belonged to the Left. At that time he'd also written about a trial of communists, in which the President had been involved. He'd mentioned the future statesman in laudatory terms, and in later years this article was frequently quoted on State occasions. On the other hand, it was said of the old writer that he had a critical stance towards the regime. In private, probably. There were no public pronouncements from him, either against or for the regime. What his reputation rested upon wasn't clear to Stirner. It was quite enough anyway for someone not to declare themselves publicly for the regime; that was seen as oppositional. Anyone who kept silent was against. The old writer had paid his dues: back in forty-nine he'd published a poem with the title 'The Shield of Peace' at the height of the Stalinist peace campaign. Later on: perhaps a bit of slave-speak, with subversion between the lines. For a few initiates. And for the experts from the Securitate, the most attentive readers. He sat there, like a symbol. A symbol of what? Of resistance, of decency, of adaptation. Probably of all this at once. Had his table, was treated with respect, sat there, looked on.

You had to flirt with the waitress in order to get anything at all. She had a way of moving about between the tables as though she didn't see a soul. And as though she didn't hear anything either. You could give an order and be convinced that she'd taken no notice – she certainly wouldn't have reacted in any way. Yet it could be that half an hour later she'd bring you what you wanted. There were even moments when she'd get involved in short conversations, make comments that could be ascribed to a particular kind of humour. Insinuations, equivocal ones. This was a clear mark of acceptance. She was extremely ugly, around fifty or so, her get-up resembled that of a waitress in the workers' canteens of the fifties. That was the time of her youth, and there were people who claimed that for a while she'd been a student of letters, at that Stalinist institute where young authors were taught the literature of the five-year plan. But she'd failed there. It was simply that a minimum of talent was required even for the Stalin literature. But she'd still be capable of writing reports for the Securitate, someone had said.

If Antonescu had halted on the Dniester, said the writer at the end of the table again, but nobody was listening to him. A young woman author began to tell Stirner about her new book. The manuscript had been gathering dust for four years. Meanwhile she'd changed publishers. The first publisher had given up. The director of this firm, a man who as she put it had been everything, from the Iron Guard through Stalinism to what he was today, had told her that she, the author, could be proud. There were lots of people who claimed to have written unpublishable books, but she really had written an unpublishable book. Now it was at the printers. The condition, in the end, had been that the book must have peace as its basic theme. So the editor had inserted the word 'peace' here and there in the text. Arbitrarily. Some of the peace passages, two or three, came from her own work. Those ones she'd accepted. It's defensible, she said. The others she'd tried to take out again at the proof stage. Now the book was stuck at the printers. There was no paper there.

Suddenly Stirner heard someone bawl out: *Adu-mi un vin, jidanule*. Stirner turned round. It was a well known film actor who'd shouted the words. He was drunk. He'd stood up and gone over to the head waiter. This actor liked playing in films about the fanatical Iron-Guardists of the forties. He was now

36

speaking just as he did on screen. You couldn't tell whether it was an act or his opinion. *Să-mi aduci un vin, jidanule*, he repeated. Fetch me some wine, Jew.

On scraps of paper he'd write down book titles from German catalogues, or from the cultural pages whenever anyone brought him a West German newspaper. Perhaps somebody might be able to send him the books one day. Friends used to come, take books from their bags, or newspapers, then hunt for something on his shelves. Got anything new? A parcel would arrive, a book would be missing. He'd note down in little notebooks what he'd loaned out. It had grown into a system, exchanging the books you owned, passing them on to be read. Books, newspapers. That way you had the impression you could break out of your isolation.

In the lift there'd once been a mirror. One day it had gone. Unscrewed. Since then there'd been no mirror in the lift. And no one asked about it either. The buttons on the control panel in the lift were provided with floor-numbers. One day these figures were rubbed off. Who'd done it was a mystery. The residents of the building wrote the figures back on again. But the next day they'd gone again. If you alluded to what had occurred, people usually said: Children, it was children. And that was the end of the matter. No one wrote the figures on again, so no one could obliterate them either. You'd enter the lift and count the buttons before pressing one. And the mirror, had there ever really been a mirror?

S tirner looked out of the window. The queue behind the
shop was still there. There were eggs. A whole truckful
must have come in. They'd been standing there for hours
already. You got twenty per person. Once someone had his
twenty, he'd immediately take up his place again. For the
next twenty. Stirner looked at a balcony in the apartment
block opposite, second floor. A young woman was taking in
her washing from the line. He'd often seen her before. She
had long, black hair parted in the middle. She was too old for
that hairstyle, and her skirts looked like young girls' skirts of
ten years ago. She had the rough gestures of a housewife and
moved about steadily on over-thin legs. He'd seen her before
in the street as well, with two children and once with her
husband. He was powerfully built, with a trace of the athlete
about him but already overweight, a ruddy beer-drinker's
face, the self-satisfied look worn by enterprise bosses, mid
thirties, Stirner's age.

Down below, in the entrance to the apartment block, hung the letter boxes in a long row on the wall, unsightly, dark-brown boxes. On top, a slot for inserting the mail; in front, above the little peep-hole, the nameplate or flat number; underneath, a little removable board furnished with a padlock. The padlocks were of varying size and quality. Stirner and Sabine had a little Chinese lock, of the kind you could still buy in the seventies. By now there were only Romanian ones, and they weren't much use. All these locks were there not just to stop the mail from being stolen, but also because otherwise the little removable boards used to go missing. Stirner and Sabine would look into the letter boxes whenever they passed by. They'd pull open the board a little, as much as the lock allowed, so that a thin ray of light would enter the box and they could see inside, through the circular hole on the front. Perhaps they'd have some mail. On days when they were at home around lunch-time, after two, one of them would go down in the lift, perhaps some mail had arrived. Often they'd get picture postcards from friends in the West, signs that someone was thinking about them. They'd read the cards to each other, and Sabine would put the nicest ones on the sideboard, for a week or two until the next ones came. Picture postcards had been agreed upon. They get through more easily, they'd said to one another, since that lot don't have to open anything first before they can read it. Those invisible men who were everywhere, on the telephone line, at public functions, in the bread queue. Sometimes letters used to come and the enve-lope would be damaged, there'd be a stamp on it, a hypo-critical one from the post office: *Sosită in această stare.* Bilingual. *Arrivé dans cet état.* Sabine and Stirner always used to check the postmarks, to ascertain how long the letters and cards had been en route. From the Bundesrepublik the mail usually took two weeks, often even three, many letters actually spent five weeks en route. Then Sabine would say: So they've been a long time reading them again.

41

S tirner saw a Romanian film in which long episodes were set in the West. The West was filmed in Romania, and looked just as Romanians who didn't know the West might imagine it. People lived in detached houses, and there'd be a bottle of whisky on the cocktail bar. The bottle would be positioned on the counter in such a way that the spectator could recognize the label. The women would cross their legs, lean back on deep chairs, toss long platinum-blonde manes and blow smoke rings into the faces of the men. In front of them on low tables would lie packets of Kent. The men too smoked Kent; they wore jeans and asymmetrically cut jackets with lots of studs. As they talked to the women, they'd toy with gold-plated lighters. Many of them wore dark glasses. It was all about industrial espionage.

Writing, what did it still mean? Stirner was one of the tolerated authors, not forbidden, tolerated. That meant you could still publish something from time to time. Perhaps even just to show the foreigners. Look, we publish them. They aren't persecuted. We publish even that kind of thing. We certainly aren't happy about it, but it can be published. Both his last books had been slim, the texts crammed together on poor-quality paper. He didn't even know how many copies had been printed. For years the print run had no longer been given in books, so that you couldn't tell how low it was. What was stipulated in the contract was in any case not binding, and publishers would give evasive answers. The texts were printed without a break. In the estimation of the Culture Minister, a woman who'd once been a textile worker, a single poem per page could be regarded as a waste of paper. But this didn't stop single poems from continuing to appear on individual pages of books: patriotic verses, the writing apparatchiks, the poets with the right connections. All of them people to whom the Securitate had no objection. Romanian authors would tote bottles along to the printworks, then the printers would run off a few extra copies, as they put it. These were intended for the author's private use. The writers would go with their editors to expensive restaurants and split their royalties with them. For, with royalties, the situation was as follows: they could be set between a minimum and a maximum. The margin was quite wide. The editor had to fix the royalty agreement on the basis of the book's merits. So he'd propose the maximum, and the royalty would be split. The waiting time would be shortened as well by this agreement. The royalty was now the editor's money as well. There were manuscripts which lay for years in publishers' drawers. As a rule, nothing definite could ever be learnt about the reasons. Rumours grew up concerning these manuscripts. And then the author in question, who of course had been lobbying the whole time and been fobbed off with excuses, would perhaps even be received by the chief editor, and it would be indicated to him that this or that passage was unclear, this bit here should perhaps be improved and that one there really ought to be left out. It wouldn't be good if. And the publishing house couldn't assume the responsibility, right. In short, it won't do. Since censorship had officially been abolished, publication had become even more complicated. Part of the censorship powers had been transferred directly to publishers. The censorship was now called a cultural commission, and it occupied itself with supervising the work of publishers. The anxiety of the latter for their jobs had increased. They could no longer delegate everything to the censor and refer any eventual problems to him. They had to make many decisions for themselves – and there weren't any clear guidelines either. A lot of authors came to be seen by publishers as their personal enemies, simply out to take them for a ride. You had to read attentively to catch the beggars out. Otherwise the book's there and they're going round boasting about what they've got through. And then they celebrate their oppositional pronouncements at the Writers' Institute, where the walls have ears, and circulate stories about the stupidity of publishing house and censorship alike. Yes, that had to be prevented. A publisher's life was no easy one. For he wasn't even that kind of person. The trouble he took, after all, to get a good book through. But did he get any thanks for that? Not a scrap. They'd even slander him into the bargain. And hadn't there already been two attempts to remove him? Stirner's books had come out, they were in the bookshops, and they disappeared from the bookshops. Three of the five German-language publications had, as you might expect, reviewed them. He'd distributed his complimentary copies to the few friends he still had these days. Stirner didn't know who his readers were. If, let's say, six hundred copies had been sold – that was the average for volumes of poetry in the German language, for prose it was a bit more – who had bought them? There were no public readings, the book trade didn't carry out any market research. In the circle of his friends, they'd puzzled for years over the problem without finding any plausible answer. Or was it indeed the case, as one fantastic rumour had it, that books like that were bought up and pulped by the Securitate, and other books then printed with the paper? Perhaps the same kind again. Stirner resisted such interpretations. The country was full of them. Full of the most arcane explanations for what occurred on a daily basis. It was Stirner's opinion that in this way you disguised reality. A life shrouded in rumours. Everybody talked about them as though fascinated. In this way time passed and the years vanished. But the question remained: For whom were they writing?

There's the woman with the pram, Stirner said. Beside her the man with the newspaper, her husband. Outing. Sunday afternoon. Sweltering heat, Stirner said. The woman was wearing a sundress. Flowers, he said. Dark flowers. Well, she's married. The man has a bald pate, carefully combed over. In spite of his age he's slim, Stirner heard himself say. He knows it, he walks very upright. He's got on a blue short-sleeved shirt. He's wearing thick glasses. Stirner reflected. She's dark blonde, he went on. Her curls were done yesterday. Saturday curls. No, her hair isn't dyed. She wheels the white pram with measured tread. Stirner fell silent. As though the sentence were still ringing in his ears. A perambulator, in advertisements, he said quickly. They circle the block in the direction of town, the husband glances up and to his left from the back page of his newspaper, greets – without altering his posture, as Stirner pointed out – the last neighbour to cross his path. In two hours' time they'll be back again, said Stirner opening a beer.

S tirner had become a Party member at university. The
woman in charge of his group had asked him whether he
was agreeable and he'd said yes. A couple of months later
he'd been ceremoniously presented with his Party card.
Stirner always used to say that he'd joined the Party in order
to change things from inside. And that he wasn't the only one
who'd thought like that at the time. That lots of people had
believed you could do something. That at the time he hadn't
been an opponent of the regime. That the regime alone had
made him one. The times were different. If he spoke with
younger people, he'd say, it was another country. Stirner
had grown up in the years of liberalization. When he was an
adult, they began to clamp down on everything again. He'd
learnt something that was no longer needed. He was useless,
but as yet he was unable and unwilling to recognize this.
Thus began his life as an enemy of the State, long before he
himself knew it. Stirner hadn't reflected for long when he'd
been asked whether he wanted to join the Party. It posed no
great problem for him. If he thought about it now, he
couldn't get rid of the suspicion that even then there'd been a
trace of that lack of commitment with which the system
stamped all concepts. He recalled how long his father had
shirked joining the Party. Stirner was a child, his father's
behaviour had been incomprehensible to him. He belonged
to another generation, had grown up in another mind-cast.
For a long time he remained the captive of this mind-cast. A
part of his life was absorbed by it. This country had had to
undergo the grotesque development of the last decade before
Stirner could find his way out of it. Until a certain moment in
time, he'd so to speak gone along. Party member, what did
that actually still mean? An entry in one's personal file
without which, for example, you couldn't become a journalist. Stirner had become a journalist, and what had he
achieved by it? Party membership had been no use to Stirner
at all, he'd just been a Party member, a statistical problem,
like a great many other things in this country.

When the sun shone, they all had to swig beer. They'd buy it by the crate. Always had some excuse. Every week some saint's day to celebrate, and between saints a football match. Because of which I've got to stand in line for my quota of beer. Stirner was furious. Because the sun's shining, I have to stand in line. On account of those saints and that football of theirs. No sport satisfies me like football, he heard someone saying. That's the kind you always get standing in front of you. Or they come straight up and stick themselves in front of you in the queue and say they were there earlier. Just been home for the bottles. At least three of them confirm it. All knew each other. Without bottles you got no beer, of course. It's hot behind the shop, midday sun. The one who's just got here wipes his mouth contentedly. Was back home guzzling, right, what else. May as well save your curses. The queue in front of you is getting longer and longer. They all know each other, right. The other day one woman arrived carrying a baby, simply went to the front, like for milk. Since when do babies drink beer then, someone called out, but she didn't let that bother her. Stirner looked at his watch. He'd been waiting forty minutes. In this sun. On account of this beer. But could he leave now, after forty minutes? From time to time he'd glance behind him, he was still one of the last. The saleswoman called through the door: Another fifteen crates. Somebody counted. It would get to Stirner. That'd really be all I needed, he thought. He tried not to think at all. It made him irritable. In front of him somebody was going on at a woman, in that heavily humorous proletarian tone of voice. The woman burst out laughing, she nodded several times in agreement. Her hair was dyed blonde. Her hairline gleamed darkly through. She was wearing a red house-dress. The humorist had on a tracksuit. Shouldn't we get a little game up, over there in the park, he called out to a man who was just leaving with a crate of beer on his shoulder. Has to get home to his wife, he added. I can get you a switch like that, he told the blonde

48

woman. We've got some. I don't have any problems with the boss. Soon it was their turn. Three more crates, called the saleswoman. A cracking good frost's what we need here, thought Stirner in his fury. Then they'd stick to swigging schnapps.

Then there was that cautious kind he couldn't stomach. They always used to find some chic way of popping subversive ideas into their poems. A type like that would still be speaking between the lines about what was common knowledge. The line would run: 'In the queue I saw a rose.' And the reader would say: Aha. That's telling them. A good book. He'd show the line to a friend, another reader. This one would say: Marvellous. The book would sell. It would be talked about. The best-known reviewers would review it in their columns, they'd quote the line and other similar ones – without commenting on them, of course. You certainly couldn't inform on the man. And anyway, they'd sigh, a literary critic has a far harder time. As a critic, you can't speak through images. The editor would say: I made this book, and his eyes would shine. The publishing house would still be a trifle anxious, there was too much talk about the book, hopefully there wouldn't be any rumpus, at least we've shown courage. People would shake the author's hand conspiratorially. The next day there'd be a little article by him in the newspaper, with his signature anyhow, as part of some campaign that was just then going on – for peace, against the destruction of folklore, for the 'four-child-family' – a clever little article that stood out agreeably from the usual sycophantic formulae, but which of course contained his approval for the campaign. How can he help it, after that book he couldn't do anything else. Then the book would be reviewed by Radio Free Europe, and the readers would say, You see, and those who didn't already own it would get hold of it at the black-market price. The proud author would tremble a little, as would his publisher: If only nothing happens now, Radio Free Europe's always the definitive confirmation, the absolute yardstick, but they still shouldn't be shouting so loudly. Because. A few days later another guarded article by the author would appear, containing his full approval for something. He's got to now, of course, the readers would say. There'd already be rumours that the book was going to be withdrawn. At all events, its black-market price would rise considerably. The author would already be working on a new book.

He saw a man. The man was standing with his back to him. The man was standing with a woman. Stirner could see just the woman's legs. The man was taller and broader than the woman. Stirner walked slowly past them. The woman's legs were held tightly together. So you could see her legs in the gap between the man's legs. They were standing very close together, closer than was necessary just to talk to each other. The man's forehead was concealed by his cap, he was speaking in a low voice but loquaciously, a smile hovering on his thin lips. The woman was clutching a folder to her chest, with both arms. She listened to him, her head was tilted up to him and her eyes were shining. Stirner had the impression that next moment she'd press up against the man and his member would penetrate her and they'd go on talking.

He was thirty-four, as old as his father had been when Stirner came into the world. He pondered this. To no avail. He was sitting at home with his parents. Summer had warmed the house. They sat at the table, the Budapest television service was just about to begin. Today's the twenty-second, his father said suddenly. It's been thirty-four years today since Matzi was drowned. Matzi, it seems, had been Stirner's cousin. No body had ever been found, his father said. The village doctor had said it was on account of the inoculations. What kind of inoculations, asked Stirner. On account of the pneumonia, said his father, as he was washed away at once. How come, pneumonia, asked Stirner. He'd always lain about half the day under the trees, on the cold ground, said Stirner's father. There was nobody at home. Your aunt was at work. He drowned in front of the inn, where there's all that coarse gravel. They're dredging there now. For sand. He wanted to go to the cinema that day, you see. But he didn't have any money. So he went to the river with the children. He was second in his class. Stirner's father fell silent. The Budapest television service began with advertising. The word *aruhaz* stuck in Stirner's mind for a time. On the screen a rustling tree appeared, slowly a girl lay down on her back. She was wearing a thin white dress. A hairspray appeared in the picture.

One day Stirner found a letter from his office in the letter box. Since you. Failed to comply. And also. Not. Your. Tasks. We can see. No other solution. Than. To dispense. With. Your services. From the first of December. We are leaving you free to hand in your own notice. If you fail to do this, we shall be obliged. According to Paragraph. To dismiss you. Stirner decided to hand in his notice. He wrote in Romanian, official language. Because my literary activity can no longer be combined with my work as an editor. So that I can pursue my literary work more effectively. He didn't write the real reasons. He lost his way in allusions. He was hoping to find another post. He was still hoping for some perspective. He still didn't want to believe that it was all over. He was hoping he'd be able to go on working in this country.

He walked for a long while. He learnt afresh how it felt to be dazzled. He walked until the smells changed. He walked about between the apartment blocks. They were built so close together there was space between them only for many-angled passages that were just like secret approaches and supply routes. He wouldn't have been surprised if a cave had suddenly lain before him. One of the pathways actually did bear the sign: *Intrarea pesterii*, 'Cave Passage'. It was a cul-de-sac. The street names were dreamed up in the offices of the town council, by people who'd never seen the neighbourhood. With their courtyards and fences and dogs, the isolated houses which had been left standing among the blocks looked like the fortifications of the last defenders. And yet they were nothing but the visible evidence of the bribes the town council had taken. He saw the shell of a factory, a half-demolished works building from the turn of the century. Though its brick walls started off in every direction only to stop short, the effect produced was nevertheless reassuring. It was an old-fashioned picture, still typical during his childhood. He saw children vanishing into dark doorways, running over the mound of rubble. Little brushwood fires blazed among the free-standing walls. A silent man headed for them. When, at about five in the afternoon, Stirner crossed the intersection in front of the sports hall, it was so quiet he could no longer hear the steps of the passers-by. He was reflecting on this as he proceeded on his way. All of a sudden he was confronted by two fiercely gesticulating deaf-mutes. Because he was sauntering across the park alone, courting couples looked at him sharply and women gave him a wide berth. For the first time this year he put on his sunglasses, old brown ones with small round lenses, a pre-war pair Sabine had bought for him at the flea market. The alien light of the sunglasses enveloped him. In the park there were stray dogs in the bushes. They held their noses close to the ground. Two militiamen were checking the papers of a young man sitting on a bench. They rummaged

55

in the grip he'd placed beside him on the bench. On another bench, children sat. They were talking like grown men. As he passed he heard a child say: *Da ce teanc de bani a avut, mă!* He'd got a whole wad of money, man! Stirner left the park. He halted at a bus stop. He reached for the note-pad in his jacket pocket. A wedding procession drew near, on its way from the registry office. There was no sign of a bus. The wedding guests continued irresolutely on their way. Irritably the bride positioned the bridegroom's clumsy arm so that she could slip her own through it. Now they were back at the head of the procession. Stirner gave up waiting. He walked down the street. A car drove by. It had *Institutul de medicină legală* written on it. Forensic medicine. After a while another arrived from the opposite direction. *Laborator criminalistic*, he read. At the next corner he turned into a side street. He walked faster. A girl was coming towards him. When he looked at her, she dropped her eyes to the ground. She was wearing a red headband. Behind a fence a dog barked at him, as if through force of habit. In a quiet street, in which elderly people were leaning from their windows and calling out Hungarian words to one another, two young men overtook him. They were talking in expert tones about octane ratings. The gist of what they were saying was that the State was cheating them on the octane rating, but they'd found this out. Their bearing was very self-assured. On a lamppost in front of a school was scrawled in red chalk, and all in one word: *Tiamo*. In the yard pupils were playing football and squabbling. They squabbled, but they went on playing. The game grew more and more violent. On the grass beside the pavement lay a man, one of the kind with whom you never know if they're drunk or have just had a heart attack. But since everyone assumes they're drunk, they're left lying there. Stirner turned into the avenue that ran alongside the Bega. He went slowly down the steps. He saw the water close at hand. It was calm. Stevie Wonder flashed into his mind. He thought about Sabine. Two-oared

56

boats rocked on the water. He heard athletes' voices. Strapping girls carried skiffs and oars to land. They moved like building workers. At the boathouse, a novice was sitting in a rowing trainer. She was endeavouring to execute oar-movements in accordance with the rules, while real boats glided past her. She looked away and continued to row clumsily. Stirner walked past the boathouse like someone who'd lost his rudder. On the masonry-lined bank, a courting couple sat upon the stone steps. The steps went down to the water, continued beneath the water. Noisy girls rode bicycles along the bank. Inexplicable feelings of happiness accompanied him. Humming old ditties he approached the town centre. In an outdoor café, he saw a man and woman sitting at a table. The man was trying to light a cigarette, but the woman kept blowing out his match. She was roaring with laughter. Stirner plucked a leaf from a bush and sniffed at it. He thought he could hear the solemn tolling of bells from Josefstadt. But then came the stutter of the tram over the rails. Young women with headscarves walked past, pensively eating dough cakes. The town was full of schoolgirls. On the first day of school, despite their uniforms, they still had that provocative holiday gait. He kept his eyes fastened on them. He felt no sense of arousal. Everywhere he saw the faces of people he knew. He dreaded any encounter. At the last moment he'd realize with relief that it was some stranger. He saw the face of a laughing girl. It was the face of Janis Joplin. On the wall of a house was written in chalk: *Nu mai fumaţi, porcilor!* Give up smoking, you pigs! The fact that the lights turned to red just as he arrived at the pedestrian crossing he felt was aimed at him. In an empty butcher's stall, a militiaman stood leaning on the counter and chatting with the butcher. Resist obvious interpretations. One sixteen-year-old girl had a mourning band on her collar. Girls ran into the cathedral and lit slender, yellow candles. The exams were drawing near. He glanced into a bar, met silent, staring looks. In the subway in front of the Opera House, at the dark newspaper kiosk papers were being sold by the light of a pocket torch. Beside the entrance stood men who stared in front of them. They were waiting for the sports paper. When he was back at street level, he saw young people coming towards him. They wore shiny black blouses. On their chests, in big letters with an exclamation mark, was written: *Da!* Yes. What did they mean by that, he wondered. In a country where for ages already everyone had been saying yes to everything. He stationed himself in the vicinity of people talking. In this way he came into possession of worthless banalities. The International of eating and drinking, conflict and hatred, envy and jealousy, weddings and funerals, had seemingly established its sections everywhere. He'd sought the meaning of the world in the street, and thus discovered the gutter in people's heads. He crossed the roadway with exaggerated caution. He had no confidence in those car-driving scoundrels. He considered them capable of anything, like horsemen on their steeds. They bore some resemblance to cowboys, with the same barbaric self-assurance. He looked away, he looked far away from himself. He no longer knew. This he knew. He must do something. Something that was capable of changing everything or that at least had the appearance of doing so. He walked on. In the little park beside the law courts sat people with doom-laden faces. He boarded the trolleybus. The bus was full. He remained standing beside the door. He didn't punch his ticket.

His insight was a cliché. Common knowledge. That when you're writing, self-censorship's the worst danger. He'd known it, of course. But you always think about that kind of thing only in relation to other people. You'd read: Aha! he's backing off there, self-censorship! You wouldn't apply it to yourself. Because you saw through it, right. As though self-censorship were a rational occurrence. As though it happened naturally, this skirting round things. Self-censorship's a virus, you carry it within you. Have done for ages. You write, and the virus writes as well. Slowly eats its way into the text. It had become clear to him that self-censorship was deep inside him. He knew it, he had to free himself from it. And he could do so only by writing. He realized there were words and thoughts which no longer came into his mind at all when he wrote. And he hadn't noticed it. He had to learn again to write those words, to think those thoughts, no matter where it might lead. So everything he wrote was a writing exercise. He had to learn to write afresh.

He saw a man and a woman, elderly people, meet another man of the same age. The woman and the man had a pedigree dog with them. The pedigree dog was behaving like a mongrel. They're people who used to keep mongrels, Stirner thought instinctively. The woman was talking to the dog as though to a child. The dog shouldn't pester people, that wasn't nice. The man wanted to show the other man how clever his dog was. He said *mort* several times, but the dog made no move to lie down and play dead. It's because my wife keeps interrupting, the man said.

He caught himself opening newspapers just to read the authors' names beneath the idiotic articles and poems. For the same reason in bookshops he'd leaf through celebratory anthologies. An odd pleasure: Aha, him too. And then passing it on. Just look, the bastard. Of course, he's got an excuse. His wife's ill, his son didn't come back from abroad, they've taken away his job, his next book can't be published, it's been in the hands of the Cultural Commission for a year and a half now, yes of course he says Cultural Commission not censorship. Did you think he'd say censorship? On national holidays, and in the last few years especially on the President's birthday, Sabine and Stirner would buy the papers just to see who else had compromised themselves, and how. They'd sit with friends and read out loud to one another. This is worth reading out, they'd say, and: Look how beautifully he sings praises. One of them would read out loud, and after every couple of lines they'd burst out laughing. Stirner didn't much care for this kind of fun, but he suspected that it didn't really displease him either. He used regularly to cut these texts out and put them in folders. For later, he'd say. In case they ever again start claiming that they knew nothing.

Because Stirner wrote in German, writing for him was often like translating. He thought in German, but all round him Romanian was being spoken. And if he wished to record a dialogue, one heard on the tram, say, he had to translate it and the dialogue lost its zest. You just can't describe it, people would say in conversations. Or else that it was best left to the Romanians. But they write for eternity, of course. This was an allusion to their aureate poetry. As a writer, Stirner was a foreigner.

One morning in June Stirner entered the outdoor café on the Bega. There was bottled beer and free tables. Stirner was astonished. Such things still existed, then. The waitress was sitting on a chair beside a stack of beer. She looked bored. He went up to her, pondered, shall I take one or shall I take two, but perhaps it'll run out, he eyed the stack, then his watch, perhaps there'll be more people arriving later on, he took two. He asked whether she hadn't any glasses, and knew his question was pointless. She hadn't got any glasses. Only inside, in the bar, she said. Everyone drank from the bottle here. It was mainly wives who asked for glasses, just drinking a bit to keep their husbands company. They'd come along so their husbands wouldn't stay so long. So they wouldn't get drunk.

Stirner went over to a free table. On the water he saw oarsmen, athletes. As if they couldn't do something better with their energy, he thought. Sport, everywhere sport. People are contented, the State's contented. Everyone talks about sport instead of about the State, the State has an opportunity to broadcast its anthem to the people. Sport's the common denominator between State and population.

He sat down with his back to the stream. He saw a fat woman and a fat girl sitting at a table. Mother and daughter. They hadn't ordered anything. There was room. The girl was filling out an extensive form. The mother was dictating. Entrance exam, thought Stirner.

At the adjoining table sat four young men. They must have been sitting there for a long time already. The table was covered with bottles. Most were empty. One man was speaking. He spoke rather too loudly. He had a contusion over his right eye. Stirner knew him by sight. He was the son of an enterprise manager. He had a cushy job somewhere, in a planning institute. That kind of institute had been established, of course, simply to provide employment for the children and wives of big shots. The fellow at the table was a notorious brawler. Even now he was once again telling the story of some brawl. Stirner listened. He didn't catch everything, but that wasn't necessary either. In Buşteni, he was just saying. X's son was there too, he mentioned the name of a manager, and Y's, now he mentioned a very well known name, you know, the Minister, he stressed, they were both there. He didn't use the first names of these people, with whom he was obviously friendly. He said whose children they were, just as peasants in Romanian villages once used to say 'old so-and-so's lad'. They themselves were nothing, of course. They existed so long as their fathers existed. We sent the landlord off to bed, he went on. It was closing time, right. He laughed. Then we locked the bar up from the inside. That was some game of poker, I can tell you. Anyone who wanted to booze simply went to the bar and served himself. Straight off the shelves. Then in comes this fellow. How he managed it, I can't think. Everything was locked up after all. And gave me this. He pointed to his face.

A girl's laughter drew Stirner's attention to another table. There was a whole party of students there. Girls and boys. He saw the girl who'd laughed. She held her closed hand in front of her mouth, with the back of her hand to her lips. She listened. One of the lads was tilting his chair back. She spoke. She kept extending her fingers so they looked longer, and her gestures seemed artificial. She listened, and as she listened she drew her necklace taut with her fingers. She spoke, and constantly moved her open hands, rolled her eyes, her hand played with her long earrings, her finger twisted her ring, her fingers ran through her hair, her eyes were black and deep and glowing. At some triviality her hand made a fluttering movement. She laughed behind her hand, with her wide, narrow-lipped mouth, she stretched out her hand, threw back her head as she laughed, hid her face in her elbow. She looked up, eyebrows raised, she listened, tongue-tip shown saucily in a reproach not meant to be taken too seriously.

He saw the fat girl place a folder in a Karstadt bag.

64

Mother and daughter left. The daughter behind the mother. He followed them with his eyes.

At a table at the back, under the trees, sat an old woman with dyed-blonde hair. She had on round, thin-framed spectacles. She wore an off-the-knee summer dress. She had her legs crossed. She'd positioned herself on her chair so that you could see her legs. On the table in front of her lay a white beach hat. She was talking to two men drinking beer, who were sitting with their backs to Stirner so he couldn't see their faces. One of the two men stood up and went over to the waitress. He was around forty, Stirner guessed. The man was wearing a white shirt under his open jacket, on the left-hand side at the level of his belly you could see a black tulip. Those were the shirts of fifteen years ago. Stirner studied the man. The black tulip over the increasing belly, he thought. Cloak and dagger of the emotions.

The orator came in, a lean, sinewy man with grey hair and a goatee. The orator was known to half the town. He often came to this café. He'd sit quietly at a table, sometimes alone, more often with company around him. People who wanted to be entertained. He'd have a drink, they'd pay. As a rule he'd start straight off. He'd murmur something, then suddenly begin to shout, usually a few regime slogans which he'd pronounce as if he were passing comment on them. But he didn't pass any comment on them. He'd simply juxtapose them with things you weren't used to hearing in that connection, or he'd pronounce them in such a way that you couldn't help laughing. Usually he'd sit with student parties. At the climax of his performance he used to stand up and mimic the gesticulations of an orator, but without saying he was mimicking them. Then the waitresses used to laugh too and say, with a glance at the uninitiated: He's just crazy. And the whole town used to say the same: He's crazy. There were lots of rumours about the orator. There were people who said he'd studied philosophy and in his time had been mixed up in some political affair. The Securitate had beaten him

65

up so badly he'd gone crazy. And now he had carte blanche to do as he pleased. Others claimed that a woman was to blame for everything, and occasionally someone would ask: How come they really let him talk? Yes, how come. Stirner had also heard it said that the orator had himself been a Securitate officer in his youth, in the fifties, and had just cracked up. No wonder, with what was going on then.

The orator had sat down at a table. He toyed with his fingers, like a person who was waiting for something and didn't know how to while away the time. Now and again he'd look up. He had a piercing gaze, which people instinctively avoided.

He dreamed he was at a butcher's stall. In disbelief he saw the meat hanging from the hooks. A few people were there, stood hesitantly about, there was no queue. And since there was no queue, no one quite dared to ask for anything, of course. Something was wrong here. Stirner went to the counter, pondering on whether you really got a whole kilo. He pondered briefly, then asked for a kilo of meat. There was a lot of fat on it, but that's how meat was now. The butcher cut a piece from the hook, weighed it, and wrapped it up. And only now did Stirner realize that he knew the butcher, it was an acquaintance from his childhood, he was smiling at Stirner. Stirner woke up. It was just before seven, it was still dark. Stirner went over to the window. Outside it was foggy. Yesterday had been foggy, and the day before yesterday had been foggy. What if it goes on like this, thought Stirner.

When Sabine and Stirner entered the café, only two tables were occupied. It was a quarter to one, too early really for lunch, but in half an hour it would be so full you'd no longer be able to find a free place. They used to come in groups then. It was the foreign students' café, where they converted their black-market profits into food. It was the only café in town that didn't look like a factory hall and where you could still eat a halfway decent meal. Moreover, Sabine and Stirner knew one of the waiters here. The acquaintance originated with Stirner. Their meeting was buried somewhere in Stirner's youth. The waiter too seemed dimly to recall something. They didn't speak about it. They greeted one another as acquaintances. The waiter treated them in a friendly fashion, which was by no means the rule with locals in this café. The waiters and waitresses moved among the foreigners' tables with marked obsequiousness, like bought souls.

The students used to make much of their foreign status. Most were Arabs, a few Greeks. Almost without exception male. Many of them ate here daily, a trivial expense given the black-market rate of the dollar. They were high-handed and subject to moods. Often they'd have their Romanian girlfriends with them. These were mostly from poorer regions; they used to arrive in the city seeking their fortune and let the foreigners support them. Almost all were known to the militia, and figured on certain reports. They were girls of limited culture. Most of them hadn't the faintest notion of geography. In school they'd been taught that the globe was round and that Romania was a beautiful and well-endowed country that was building socialism – under the wise leadership, what is more, of the President. Everything else was abroad. And abroad was the American films which until a few years ago used to be shown in the cinemas; the clothes from the fashion catalogues your dressmaker used to have sent; the oranges and jeans your friend might bring back: Lebanon was Paris and Jordan was America and America was neon lights and neon lights were discos and discos were leisure and leisure was music and music was beautiful. So there were girls who used to hope some student from Jordan or Lebanon would marry them, and lots did get married too, and the State would release them to Lebanon or to Jordan – after a bit of to-ing and fro-ing, to be sure, about whether there weren't any men left in Romania and so forth – and then they'd be in Jordan, in Lebanon, and that would be the end of abroad.

Sabine's and Stirner's waiter was an original. A waiter left over from another era. He'd dart hither and thither between the tables, greet everyone who came in, exchange a few words with everyone. It was his custom to address the foreign students as 'Herr Doktor'. The undertone was ironic. He used to mimic their Romanian, and if one was particularly high-handed, the waiter would take his revenge with a cryptic phrase in Hungarian, say, which the person in question wouldn't, of course, understand.

The waiter winked at Sabine and Stirner. It was the conspiratorial wink of the locals. Foreign scum! Oh, they've got money all right. But real morons. That's the way it is, what can you do. Stirner looked out of the window. He surveyed the green water of the Bega. Willows trailed in the water. On the bridge he saw people in long columns. They were carrying pictures and slogans, they were going towards the town centre. A student came in and asked the lone waitress where one of the waiters was. He's at the meeting, she said. Stirner recalled that one of those nauseating peace rallies had been arranged for today, to the further glorification of the President, best-loved son of the nation.

At the next table the foreigner's Romanian girlfriend was wrapping the leftover chicken liver in a paper napkin, with the tips of her fingers. The waitress passed by and the girlfriend slipped her a Kent.

69

After his last visit to his parents, he'd brought back with him his old stamp-glass. He'd asked whether it was still there, and his mother had said: Take it, it's in the drawer. Which drawer, he'd asked, and she'd gone over to the cupboard and pulled out a drawer and taken out the glass. Here, she'd said. It had been the same drawer from which in his day he'd always taken it himself, and the glass was still in the same case. Now it lay on a shelf in the flat. Sabine would sometimes use it for studying photos in magazines, she enjoyed the distortions, she'd hold the glass at an angle and laugh at Stalin's moustache. Stirner hadn't made any further use of it. From time to time he'd forget about it, as he would about other objects in the flat for which there was no application.

He read an old letter he'd written to Sabine nine years ago. He read it as he was tidying up, while throwing away useless old papers. He read it for no reason, out of idle curiosity. The letter was alien to him, even the handwriting was that of another person. The phrases struck him as clumsy, the tone was boastful, full of self-pity, the contents were crude and irritating. He wouldn't be able to do much with the individual writing there, Stirner thought. It was almost always in Sabine's absence that he went in for these bouts of tidying-up, as though he didn't want to be caught. He'd grab old stacks of paper, leaf through them, read, reflect, often couldn't make up his mind to throw the things away. Some of them reminded him of forgotten events, many remained mute, as though they'd never had anything to do with his life. And yet there must have been something there. It used to make Stirner uneasy. Things were eluding him. He felt as though parts of his life were slipping away from him. He was growing older, and sometimes it was as if everything behind him was being lopped off. What he was leaving behind demanded as much effort from him as what he was moving towards. It was no use accumulating papers, it was also no use tearing papers up.

He observed the radiant faces of the actresses on television declaiming the odes in honour of the President's birthday. At home they'd be grumbling about the supply of goods, he thought, about wages, the repertory, the heating, public transport, about their roles, about the ban on abortions, about this programme. He listened to their pathetic voices, and he knew that as they recited that slime they were secretly hoping the latest rumour was true, they were pinning all their hopes on it: He, the President, is sick. Soon he'll die, and then it will all be over. Stirner gazed at their shining eyes and said: You shameless bunch of zombies, with some luck you'll have him for a long while yet.

H e lay in bed. Behind him the light of the reading lamp burned. Suddenly, on the carpet, he saw the shadow of his hand. He began to make shapes, silhouettes, as in his childhood, but he no longer had any grasp of the rules of the game, so his hand's shadow produced nothing recognizable.

He was fed up with sitting at the old portable radio and searching for stations on short-wave where he might hear a few items of news. Surrounded by mere crackles, he traced meticulously how, at the same time, a huge lie emerged to cover the world. The Soviet, Titoist, Euro-Communist and Chinese revisionists, he said laughing. American imperialism. The highest stage of development. The country in which true socialism is being built. The people has faith in its leadership. Our German-language service is now closing down. The Internationale rang out. He listened to it right through to the end. Then he switched off the radio.

For years Sabine and Stirner hadn't got married. We're fine, they'd told one another, even without the State's wretched scrap of paper. That's one thing at least we're not going to have confirmed in writing. And they didn't care anyway about what their friends and relations said. But they were continually running up against the authorities' ordinances. There were difficulties everywhere. Their case was not provided for. Nor was it approved of – either by the State or by other people. In such matters, State and people were in total agreement. They could neither spend the night together in a hotel room nor travel in the same sleeping-car. The interesting thing was that intricate, corrupt and discredited as they were, such regulations were strictly adhered to. As though they constituted the entire semblance of normality without which nothing else could be sustained. It was simpler to get hold of a fake medical card and go off on holiday than to be unmarried and spend the night in a hotel room together. And that was just the tip of the iceberg. After years of this kind of thing, they were fed up with it. They gave in. They took their papers to the registry office. But getting married was by no means that simple. Since a blood test was needed, men wishing to marry were compelled to donate blood. Voluntarily. Anyone who didn't donate didn't get the certificate. Stirner refused, and the only way out was to bribe a doctor. Sabine and Stirner went to the registry office alone. They went in their everyday clothes. At the registry office, the officials asked where the bride and groom were then, and whether they didn't want any photos. They were conducted to a hall. The registrar wore a sash in the national colours. He was standing behind a low table, upon which – in one of those standard files utilized by the militia, the housing office and doctors – their papers lay. He told them to stand in front of the table, a bit closer together, he said, then in a kind of mumble he quoted a bit from the marriage law. After seeming to hunt around for a theme, he then found one and came down to particulars: it was primarily concerned with

75

the future husband, who was evidently regarded as quite capable of leaving wife and child in the lurch; the child figured in his script from the outset, as though it had been written by the Catholic Church. The registrar stared straight between them with his watery blue eyes and pronounced them man and wife. All they had to do now was go into a little office and sign their names. When they were back outside, they saw the wedding parties waiting in front of the registry office: anxious mothers, bustling fathers, serious young men in light-coloured suits, happy brides. The cars were adorned with flowers, the photographers were already scurrying up. Preparations for something. Sabine and Stirner travelled to the centre of town. They went for a meal in a restaurant. It was a Tuesday. The meal was bad.

From the kitchen window you could see the district hospital, a uniform concrete-grey tower block. Nine floors, eight of them with bars on the windows. No gardens. The visiting days were Thursdays and Sundays after three, you'd see people making their way to the hospital with heavy bags. In front of the building old women sold flowers and apples. They didn't have licences, but the militia left them in peace. At around five the people would leave the hospital again. Their bags would be light. On Sunday afternoons in summer, patients would often stand on the flat roof of the hospital. These were the football fans. From up there you could see into the stadium next door. How tiny the players must be. Behind the hospital was a stretch of open ground, and behind this a new housing estate had been built: apartments with linoleum floors and windows so small that it was dark in the rooms even in daytime. The people who lived there had trodden a path diagonally across the open ground. Their appearance and dress betrayed their rural provenance. In the shops the most ill-assorted things were displayed side by side, just as you find in the country. The people had laid out little gardens between the apartment blocks. The President had suggested in a speech that the areas between apartment blocks should be planted with vegetables. That a great deal of land was lying fallow there. He'd evidently been expressing his predilection for elementary-school arithmetic. The people didn't wait to be asked. Everybody seized their few square metres of ground and, as a sign that it belonged to them, fenced the rectangle in. People used to potter about on these patches as if they owned a whole hectare of land. The housing estate was flanked by a little wood, in which Stirner used sometimes to go for a walk. Behind the wood three rural farmsteads still survived. Leftovers that the steamroller of the city hadn't yet reached. Dogs would be heard barking. Stirner would gaze across the empty fields. On the way back he used to walk past the hospital, and once he saw children standing by the

77

fence that enclosed the hospital yard. They were staring at a minibus in the yard; its rear doors stood ajar, but at an angle such that Stirner was able to see inside only when he arrived at the same level as the bus. From the interior of the vehicle there jutted a black coffin.

In his dream he repeatedly penetrated a woman, but was unable to recognize her face. So he woke up. He turned on the radio, and was at once surrounded by the jingles of his childhood. He hovered between laughter and sadness. Severing the umbilical cord from his parents' worthy existence had been an easy matter. The pull of knowledge and the world sucked him almost unawares into a maelstrom of perplexities shrouding an unattainable glimmer. Suddenly from the radio came *Talking 'bout my generation*. He passed his hand over his forehead, but the skin there felt so thin that he stopped. He switched on the bedside lamp. His gaze fell on the posters hanging on the wall. There they were, his failed models. He looked at them and grew insecure. Wasn't it merely chic, in fact: just pinning up all those radicals on his wall, all those individuals who'd died young, those misfits, those victims of torture, those dissenters? Wasn't it simply a parading of opinions and attitudes? See, visitor, that's the kind of person I am. I, the radical-for-fun. I, the progressive survivor of those who died young. Anyhow, his way of life wasn't described by them. He came across like a fan. He lay awake. His hand was lying so far away that he was frightened he wouldn't be able to touch himself again. Somewhere in the building, an alarm rang.

His employment book arrived in the mail. It had *plecat la cerere* recorded in it – 'at his own request'. Now he was out of work. A term that officially didn't even exist in this country. You were without a post, or temporarily jobless. Or not in employment. And that was already covered by a paragraph of the legal code. Parasitism. Work-shy. This paragraph was also brought to bear against awkward people, mainly against members of the neo-Protestant sects whose number had risen sharply in recent years. At first they'd be dismissed under some pretext, a pretext could always be found, then they'd be accused of parasitism. When Stirner was asked about his work, he'd usually say he was a freelance writer, and if people looked at him strangely he'd continue: Member of the Writers' Union. 'Writers' Union' was a term that even the militia accepted. It still retained a discernible glimmer of the power the Union had once enjoyed under Stalinism. Now, though, it was in the process of degenerating into a mere sender of congratulatory telegrams to the President, like other social organizations before it. We the writers of Romania. Stand four square behind your new initiative. Stirner applied to the Union leadership for a post. The president received him – after a certain amount of to-ing and fro-ing; one time he wouldn't be in, another time he wouldn't have time – and listened to him, took some notes in a little book of the kind Party officials used, and eventually promised that they'd clarify Stirner's situation. This was how he put it. He looked at Stirner with empty eyes. That was the end of the interview. The Union president was a busy man. It occurred to Stirner that he'd fully internalized the gestures of an official. Yet he was regarded as a considerable novelist. Since taking up his office, at any rate, he hadn't written any more novels. That was always how it went. They'd write, be published, become famous, be awarded the positions – and nothing else would appear. They'd turn into components, cogs in the system of general repression. They participated in power; though they

80

had absolutely no belief in it, they were nothing but stamp-wielders and signature-artists. They'd been caught up in the vast hotbed of intrigue that the Union represented, in which only intelligence reports were written and only informers' reports read. And Comrade Colonel would drop in for coffee.

He dreamed he had a glass eye, and with this glass eye you could see. He saw with it, but it was impossible for him to say what he saw. He saw, if he really had to put a name to it, he saw a feeling. And this feeling was black. Impossible to make out anything more definite, he said in his dream, for he was talking to somebody, though to whom he couldn't say. The person was known to him, but had no name. Stirner woke up in a kind of certitude that made him insecure. If he'd had to say now what he'd seen, he wouldn't have been able to describe it. Was it important, Sabine asked. It was important, Stirner said. But I don't know anything any more. I don't know anything at all.

For financial transactions Stirner would usually go to the little savings bank next to the Lacto-Bar. He'd discovered years ago that there weren't many people there in the morning before nine. You didn't have to queue. This time just two old women were there. Stirner went to the window at which, according to the sign, his business had to be transacted. A girl who'd been doing something there went off without favouring him with so much as a glance. She left the room as though she hadn't seen him. At both the other windows sat women of around forty. They were wearing the multiple sweaters of all office ladies. The premises were unheated. One of them was reading something with intense concentration from a sheet of paper. A young woman came in and sat down behind Stirner's window. He held out his request. She rummaged through some documents and at the same time struck up a conversation with her colleague, who was still staring at the paper. There was no way of knowing whether she'd noticed Stirner. She stretched out her hand in Stirner's direction. He handed over his documents. She glanced briefly at them and began filling in data with a fountain pen. She consulted a register, then made a lengthy entry in another register. Every so often she'd laugh in amusement. Her colleague was leaning across towards her and reading odd passages aloud from the sheet that had been absorbing her all this while. Stirner listened for a time. It was a horoscope, probably translated from a West German magazine and duplicated on a typewriter.

83

He came home and from force of habit went to the letter box in the hall. He saw a woman who lived on the sixth floor coming down the stairs, and was surprised. Aha, he thought, no electricity again. All the same he went over to the lift and pressed the button, but the light didn't go on. He climbed up the stairs, swearing quietly to himself. People passed him on the dim staircase. There were voices on the landings. He couldn't hear what they were saying. He didn't look at the people he encountered, he barely greeted them. He felt as if they were all responsible for the situation, as if they were part of it.

S ince he'd lost the habit of going out in the evenings, it had
become distasteful to him if he did ever have to leave the
house. The dark city, the hurrying people. It was like the
depths of a depression. As he walked, he couldn't rid himself
of the feeling there was something wrong with his sense of
balance. He walked like a prisoner in a walled-in enclosure
from which you could see nothing but the sky. You were
outside, yet you saw nothing of the outside. It had already
been years now since he'd stopped going out in the evenings.
Where should he go anyway? At the cinemas the last performance was at eight, and the kind of films they were! And you
should see the people who went to them. Every time there
was a death on the screen they'd roar with laughter. He'd
always been a morning cinema-goer anyway. He used to love
stepping out of the dark cinema into the bright street.
Because of the power cuts, only a few cinemas still had
morning performances. The films shown were mostly
Romanian, Korean, Indian and Chinese, every so often a
Soviet one. Occasionally perhaps some old American action
film would find its way into a cinema. People had grown used
to it. They'd queue up now for Chinese and Indian films just
as they'd once done for American and French ones. Only
Soviet films they steered clear of, now as before. Why should
Stirner go out in the evenings? The restaurants closed at
nine, you could get nothing anyway except low-grade roast
meat and low-grade white wine, and if you visited friends
you had to be forever looking at your watch so you wouldn't
miss the last tram. And you'd be none too sure that was
running, either. And friends? How many did you still have?
Most of them had emigrated, and with the ones who were left
there were considerable differences of opinion. Quarrels
would break out, helped by plenty of alcohol, as if you had to
settle all the State's woes between yourselves. As if you were
responsible for it all. It was the pressure of events that put a
strain on relations. Why should Stirner leave home in the
evenings? There was something else, which he didn't like

85

putting into words. How quickly one could have an accident. Hadn't somebody been fished out of a lake just recently, and no one knew how he'd got there. He'd been buried and that had been the end of it. Quietly, so to speak. Everything took place quietly here. Each day some quiet crime would occur, and nobody cared. Stirner used to say he didn't have a persecution complex but, on the other hand, that didn't stop him from being careful. He stayed at home in the evenings. He talked to Sabine. He'd sometimes say this was really enough for him. They were in agreement about most things. But the heightened degree of companionship wasn't rooted solely in their relationship; part of it was to be attributed to pressure from the system. They loved one another, and they felt solidarity with one another. They'd built their barricades against the situation. But this operated like a cancer. Quarrels always had something to do with the situation. It had become difficult to distinguish between a living relationship and a relationship of survival. In the evening, when the reception was good, they'd sit in front of the television set. They'd watch Belgrade and Novi Sad, and this television viewing preserved a relationship with images of the outside world. They'd seen films here over the years about which otherwise they'd have known only by hearsay. They listened to the radio, just Western stations, whenever you could get them; and the Austrian Broadcasting Service, for example, had become indispensable to them for its cultural programmes. They lived as if in Korea, but this Korea was located in the Balkans and access to the outside world could, with a bit of effort, be maintained. So their heads were full of images of that other world in which they didn't live but about which they knew, and their dissatisfaction grew.

The leaves in the park were of a strident yellow. In the morning no one was there and Stirner, emerging from the traffic, saw how stiff the trees were. How motionless. Leaves were falling from one tree, and Stirner kept an instinctive eye open for the person responsible. But there was nobody there. Under the tree, propped against the undergrowth, he saw a bicycle. He stopped, but couldn't see the bicycle's owner. He walked a bit further along the path and, when someone approached, kicked at the dense blanket of leaves covering the asphalt. The path ran alongside a high wire-netting fence, over which hung creepers that blocked one's view of the area behind the fence. At two points, however, there were wide gaps in the foliage. Most passers-by would stop here for a while and peer through the fence. From inside you could hear a dry thud at short, regular intervals. And terse commands in a masculine voice. Angry abuse: You're either an idiot or a cretin. How many times have I told you to hold the racket tighter. Stirner walked through the park in a broad loop. Then he turned round. He gazed across the open parkland. Beside a tree stood a young woman with a huge wolfhound. She was attaching a plastic bag to the trunk. The dog was leaping round her. Otherwise there was no one to be seen. At short, regular intervals you could hear a dry thud.

No, this poem won't do, said the director. The publishing house was located in a little building in the back yard of the Party school. The servants must have lived here in the old days. If you wanted to visit the publishing house, you had to go past the porter and the Party school. Anyone wishing to go to the Party school would be checked at the gate. Anyone going to the publishing house would simply call into the porter's lodge: 'For the publishing house' and be let through at once. This poem absolutely won't do, said the director. Stirner was sitting in his cramped office. You mention Odessa in it. The director used the Romanian form *dumneata*, which is untranslatable. It oscillates somewhere between the intimate and formal modes of address. It can be familiar, but also disparaging. This time there was a hint of familiarity. Or even a mixture of both. Why shouldn't I mention Odessa, said Stirner. The director cleared his throat, groaned, glanced around as though someone might hear him, then resolved to answer all the same. He leaned forward slightly, his voice was lowered: In Odessa we Romanians really did cause havoc, you see. An imperceptible light came into his eyes. Odessa, the Eastern Front. No, that won't do. All right then, said Stirner. How about this? He handed the director a sheet across the table. The director read it, then said: Without the last line. But that's the whole point of the poem. Without the last line, the director repeated. It's clear there who you mean, isn't it? Then let's leave the poem out, said Stirner. But how about this one? He handed another sheet across the table. The director looked at the poem. Then he looked at Stirner and smiled, like a person who has spotted someone attempting to slip one across him. This line here. In a strong Romanian accent he read: Red Flags, Red Figures. Well, that won't do, will it. But whatever's wrong with this one? It came out in the newspaper. The newspaper's not the same thing as a book, said the director. In a newspaper poems appear in isolation, in a book they complement each other, the context provides additional nuances. And anyhow, all kinds of stuff gets published in the newspapers. But it was published in the Party paper – Stirner stuck to his guns. Isn't that binding on you? At this point the director grew indignant. Stirner had struck the wrong note. It was clear even to him that his question had been unfair. It had been one of those little instances of petty blackmail. With it, Stirner had ventured onto terrain which he normally fought against. He said he'd sacrifice the poem. The director remained sullen. He seemed to regard the interview as terminated. Just one more, said Stirner and handed the sheet across the table. This one too, said the director. He again quoted in German: Language of murderers. How can you write that, as a German. Now he really got going. That disturbs me. Me personally. He was quite an admirer of German culture, as people used to say. If you leave out that phrase, the poem can stay in. Let's leave the phrase out, Stirner said.

S tirner entered an outdoor café. It lay on a slope. He saw a counter in the open air. At a table sat friends who greeted him and asked whether he was coming to the wedding on Saturday. Stirner didn't understand this. It must have happened long ago. He went to the counter, and was surprised nobody was queuing. Two beers, he heard himself say hesitantly. Forty-three Lei, said the waiter. It's foreign, he added. Stirner studied the bottles, there were no labels stuck on them. Look there, the waiter pointed to a carton. It's Polish, he said. But Stirner couldn't make anything out. He woke up.

Everywhere, including in the field of literature, the posts were held by people who'd soon be drawing pensions. They'd been young in the fifties. Back in Stalin's day. They'd wept at meetings when Stalin died. They'd survived. So what had their role been from '57 on, in the second wave of repression? Well, they'd already been occupying minor, inconspicuous positions with excellent prospects. They weren't victims. Witnesses? In the second half of the sixties, during the liberalization, they seized power. Since then they've held the key jobs. Feathered their nests. Sit there in their villas. Where the bourgeoisie used to sit. Can no longer imagine things being different. Cling to their seats. As though they had cramp. Can't do much any more, as they put it. They'd very much like to help you, but. Things aren't how they used to be any more. You could still find a niche for someone in those days. Back then, when everybody was coming out of gaol. No, nothing's going right any more. Their celebratory articles pile up. One embarrassment after another. They wouldn't be sorry if the whole lot were to vanish overnight, whole mountains of newspapers and archives dissolving into thin air. Alas, that wasn't possible. So they shouldered the burden of their lives, and would sometimes pour out all their troubles to you. Meanwhile their children lived abroad. Had cleared out during a trip to the West. Aren't tough enough for the socialism of their parents. There they sat now, in the heart of imperialism, and their parents, the ageing custodians of the new man, would now and again be allowed to visit them.

Stirner went to the Party committee. They made him wait, they were friendly. All right, we'll see. It's not so simple. So you don't want to go back into journalism. There's nothing going in the library field at present. He went again. Yes, we haven't forgotten you. No, but there hasn't been anything yet. There's nothing in film. You wouldn't consider a cultural centre? Well, as an organizer. Come back another time, or better still, call me. Here's the telephone number. If you happen to hear about an empty post anywhere, give me a call. We'll leave it like that then. Stirner talked to people. They listened to him. They wrote down what he said in notebooks. But he couldn't help seeing that he wasn't making any progress at all. He'd present his application, they'd nod and make promises, but somewhere there was a big invisible hand that wiped everything away. It was as though he were to write and no letters appeared on the paper. And he'd keep starting all over again, and the same thing would keep happening.

I'm going to the depot. The one for building materials, said a woman's voice to another woman's voice. Stirner was sitting, the women were standing, he was sitting with his back to them. It was cold on the tram. In November most women no longer sat down on the tram. Stirner couldn't see the two women. I need a – he didn't catch the rest. Then you need a contact in the – the next word was lost in the noise of the tram. It's cold, said one of the women's voices. Some people are already wearing furs, but it's still too early for that. You don't wear furs yet at this time of year. Yesterday first thing I wouldn't have minded having furs. It was three degrees below. The tram stopped. Stirner read the sign at the tram stop: *Parcul poporului.* People's Park. At the stop stood a man in his late thirties whom Stirner knew. It was one of those individuals who'd been offering their services to the regime for years, a regular visitor at editorial and Party offices. Among the journalists, there were people who claimed he was an informer. Others regarded him as a nutcase. He also wrote articles, you see, on historical topics to do with the Banat. His favourite field was the history of local medicine. He'd hammer away so persistently with these articles of his that eventually they'd print something just to get rid of him. For a while at least. The tram rattled on. He hadn't boarded it. I'm off to collect my boot. It's being repaired. With a bit of luck they'll have it ready today. I'm already down twenty-five Lei. The heel. I'm wearing shoes. Me too, said the other woman's voice. And how are things with you otherwise? My husband's gone off to my brother's. He's helping him with some concreting. The tram stopped again. Stirner dismounted, without turning to look at the two women.

S tirner walked through the park beside the cathedral. It was the only one in the city where the benches, for some unknown reason, were undamaged; benches dating back to the sixties, with broad planks supported by concrete pedestals. Nearby stood more recent benches, iron rods welded together, thin slats on top. In the middle of the park there was a broad avenue. Here stood the monument to the Romanian soldiers who'd fought in the Second World War, or more precisely in the final phase of the war, after the palace revolt of 23 August 1944 when Romania had switched sides. Nobody ever spoke about the first three years of war. Romania on the Eastern Front, as an ally of the Third Reich: that had never existed. That period didn't figure in the history books. Only pensioners would talk about it, as of a bygone youth, a time irretrievably past. Odessa, the Crimea, Stalingrad, what did the young people know about these?

The monument was composed of white marble blocks and stood on a tall plinth: a soldier, with flag raised high and rifle at the ready. The side reliefs showed allegorical scenes: on the left, soldiers fighting in close combat with an invisible enemy; on the right, women with flowers, workers, peasants and children thronging round the victors. Steps led up to a little platform, also of marble, on the front of the monument. On October mornings there'd be children in pioneer uniforms standing on this platform, performing the 'Pioneereid' under their teachers' direction. Patriotic poems would be recited. Songs sung. The children would pledge allegiance to the President and to the Fatherland. A short way off parents would stand, children's jackets in their arms, gazing mutely on. They'd be men and women of Stirner's age. They'd be working an afternoon shift, or else have left work. Just for a moment. At the close of the ceremony, a photographer would arrive who'd previously been standing to one side. He'd scurry up like a wedding photographer.

For a while Stirner looked on. Far away behind the monument pensioners were playing chess or cards – rummy

– on concrete tables: the people standing round them eyed passers-by mistrustfully. It was quiet, in spite of all the people, and the event had a vaguely illicit air.

Stirner walked in the direction of the Corso. On both sides of the avenue along which he was walking stood the showcases of local enterprises, with photos of the best workers. For two years now the photos had been in colour. He stared more and more insistently into the faces of the models, but they remained expressionless. Nobody looked at these photos, they were like the statues in the park, about which people knew nothing. Now and again at night the glass of one of the showcases would be smashed. Then the splinters would remain stuck in the frame for weeks, but no picture would ever be removed. On the benches between the showcases sat schoolgirls in greasy tunics. They were giggling. Stirner left the park.

S tirner's view of young people was sceptical, his comments on teenagers disparaging. He was fond of using the word 'teenager', and that said it all. He mistrusted this generation. He regarded it as superficial. As stupid. As opportunistic. This wasn't just said unthinkingly, of course. He'd got examples too. And what examples! He considered them capable of anything. The fact that they exploited their parents made him happy, to tell the truth. It was all they deserved. He himself had no children, of course. Good thing too. Them and their shining eyes: the President had once said he'd seen thousands upon thousands of young people on the country's building sites, young people with shining eyes. They were the ones who'd grown up in the years of the President's power. His own, Stirner used to say. His reaction might have been that of an elderly person. And sometimes he was even aware of this. Then he'd wonder whether he too hadn't been like that once. But he'd always find fresh counter-arguments. No, things were different then. Such thoughts made him feel quite uncomfortable.

I n November they'd felled the little wood. When Stirner arrived there one Sunday afternoon, all the undergrowth and half the trees were missing. The wood was suddenly transparent. There were scorch-marks on the grass. A smell of smoke. At any rate that was Stirner's impression. He walked along the main track. On one of the side tracks, a couple caught his eye. The man was standing in the middle of the forest trail; he was wearing a sports jacket over which he'd slung a showy square black bag. The man was standing with his back to Stirner. At first Stirner couldn't see what he was doing with his hands. The woman was leaning against a tree on the edge of the trail. She was wearing a blue-and-white checked coat, had her hands in her coat pockets, and kept thrusting her foot forward so that the coat fell open in front. As she did so, she kept her eyes on the man. She repeated these movements several times, always the leg forward, the coat half open, leaning against the tree differently on each occasion; then she tossed her curls several times and shook out her mane. The man was moving in front of her too; maintaining his distance he held a camera, which Stirner only now noticed, first over his head then in front of his chest. Stirner had kept going, so he was now looking at them both from the side. The man was signalling to the woman with his left hand as he took photographs. Stirner couldn't make out whether they were talking to one another. The woman took off the coat. Now, as the man approached, snapping away, she stood facing him in a pink sweater and tight grey skirt. He brought the camera really close up to her face, then moved away again. Stirner saw her black, high-heeled Sunday shoes. The checked coat was hanging on the tree. The camera dangled in front of the man's chest. Stirner had stopped. He saw them among the bare trees that stood so far apart. The woman had her arms folded across her chest as though she felt cold. They seemed to be talking to one another. Suddenly the woman put her coat on and they walked off very quickly, as though they'd been caught.

97

He lay in bed reading. The reading wasn't really reading. Just dipping. Sabine was in the other room. It was evening. He'd looked out of the window. Outside it was dark. A pale glow came from the illuminated windows of the neighbouring block, and the moving cars cast a short beam of light ahead of them. He'd turned on the television. In Bucharest the Sunday festival programme was showing, with poems and songs for the President. Several times there appeared on the screen in big letters: PRIMA AUDITIE. Premiere. There followed songs by well-known composers extolling peace and the President's latest peace initiative. How quickly they managed it! Stirner stopped watching for quite a while. He read: 'The consul brushed the dust from his suit; he looked in vain for injuries – not the slightest scratch.' He got up, went into the kitchen. Are you going to the kitchen again, he called to the other room. He switched out the light in the kitchen. He went into the hall, looked to see whether the front door was properly locked. He removed the key and placed it as usual on the refrigerator. He went back into the bedroom. On the television, a townscape was visible: on a broad square countless people were standing in a vast composition; dressed up as workers, peasants, soldiers, intellectuals, women, pioneers and falcons; and singing a choral ode to the President, a colossal portrait of whom hung resplendent on a tall building in the background. He switched over to the Belgrade channel, leaving the sound on Bucharest with the help of his VHF radio. In Belgrade a variety programme was showing, popular songs, dancing. He left the Bucharest sound on with this picture. It amused him. He read some more. He switched off the television set. Everything was quiet. He read. He heard creaking in the pipes. Aha, they're turning the heating on. He automatically had the same thought he had evening after evening. Perhaps this winter it won't be so cold.

The worse the situation grew, the more the campaigns proliferated. The idea was to occupy people's minds, keep them busy. They should have no time to come to grips with their situation. There were campaigns that were devoid of any popular interest, like the regular peace actions; and ones directed against popular interests, like the campaigns for saving electricity and against abortion; and ones that were approved of by sections of the population but incited these against other sections of the population, like criticism of prices on the private market or of counter-clerks. There were regular birthday campaigns for the President and for his wife; campaigns against parasitism, against mysticism, against emigration, against the hoarding of foodstuffs, against Radio Free Europe, against misuse of medicaments. One shrill note followed hard upon the heels of the last. The people appeared indifferent, but their revulsion could be told from the fact that you could no longer discuss any problem seriously with them. Sometimes Stirner would catch himself thinking how he couldn't bear the sound of the word 'peace' any more. People protected themselves by means of jokes. No sooner would the regime launch some new thesis than there'd already be the first joke about it. It was significant that the largest number of jokes used to circulate in the capital. People claimed that such jokes were swapped even in the central committee.

He travelled to the railway station. It was a quarter to seven. A woman friend was arriving. On the tram young people stood around talking to one another, as usual. Only their eyes were different. They were red-rimmed. Night-shift, it occurred to him. He rarely travelled by tram at this time of day. Three seats away in front of him, two young men were speaking German. One was sitting, the other standing. Wasn't he getting married, asked the one who was sitting. Yes, in June, said the other promptly. That's the best time to get married, said the one on the seat. June, July. Why should I wait, said the other. And aren't you going to get married? I'm still young, said the one who was sitting. Still got time.

Behind them sat a militiaman, in a blue militia greatcoat; old, with a pale face, his hair silvery-grey. He had the face of a general, and this face was staring into space. Stirner's gaze slid to his epaulettes. No star – a sergeant, of course.

As the tram crossed the station bridge, Stirner glanced to the left, to where the Yugoslav tourist buses usually stopped on the Bega Embankment. He counted seven buses. The passengers were still sitting inside them. Around the buses you could see in the half-light the growing crowd. It was Saturday. The largest number of buses used to come on Saturdays. The Yugoslavs would fasten samples of their wares to the insides of the bus windows with adhesive tape. Chocolate, cigarettes, packet soups, spices. In their arms they'd hold jeans. Through the glass there'd be haggling, in two languages, fingers would be raised. Shaking of heads, nodding. Hundreds would pass up, cigarettes down. At lunchtime, Gypsy women would stand outside the Josefstadt shops reselling the wares which they'd procured that morning. There were real bargains. Quartz watches, for example, which played seven tunes. In their hands the Gypsy women would hold tapes containing watch batteries and contraceptive pills. They'd call out: *Antebebi si batirii. Antebebi pentru fetite.* Pills for the young ladies.

The tram swept into the loop in front of the railway station and came to a halt. Stirner entered the station concourse. Round the windows that were open, people were thronging. No proper queues could be made out, just shoving, jostling crowds. What are you pushing in front for, can't you wait your turn, But my train's leaving, Ours too, I can't queue with the kid, surely you can see that, That's your husband waiting over there, isn't it, You've all got some good excuse, He might at least get a move on with the tickets, What on earth's she up to, Get one for me too, It's really something again today.

It was just before seven. On the electronic indicator, Stirner saw the advertised delay to the train. Twenty minutes. He went down to the subway, for newspapers. There were the three local papers, Romanian, German, Hungarian. The national papers arrived at about midday, or even only the following day. That depended on whether the President had delivered some lengthy speech the previous afternoon. Stirner looked carefully at the display. One of the two German-language weeklies was there too. In the subway, little groups of schoolchildren stood against the piers. They'd arrived by the early trains, it still wasn't time for school.

Stirner returned to the concourse. This time he didn't go up the steps and then along the platform; he walked through a long tunnel, from the ceiling of which thick, bare pipes were suspended. At the end of the tunnel the station lavatories were located, they could be recognized by the stench. To the right of these a staircase led up to the concourse. At the foot of this staircase sat a beggar. People had already grown so accustomed to his presence that now they scarcely gave him anything.

Stirner remained for a while in the concourse. Leaning against the wall, he read the papers. He was soon done with that. He glanced briefly at the obituaries, read a few of the classified ads: For sale new stereo cassette recorder,

101

Disposing of house contents – I see, another one emigrating – Various household objects, Exchange two-room flat for three-room flat, central, gas connection, garage, For sale foreign medicines, Wanted video recorder, Books for sale, German intellectual seeks room. He tucked the papers into his pocket. A militiaman walked through the concourse with an inquiring gaze. It was one of those young swaggerers who've seen too many police movies, pathetic little gun fetishists acting like sheriffs.

Stirner walked out onto the platform. The train must be in soon. It was already forty minutes late. He went past the office of the station militia. Beside the door stood a large showcase. Photos were visible behind the glass; under the photos, typewritten captions. They had that sarcastic police tone. Stirner looked at the photos. Two women, who according to the caption pursued the oldest profession in the world. One of them, aged seventeen, had been missing for months, anyone who saw her should inform the militia. The other, a woman of about forty, had abandoned husband and children and come to the city. In another photo a man could be seen. He was sitting at a table on which lay foreign goods, cigarettes, coffee. He'd been involved in the black market. Further photos showed men with bottles in their hands, drunk. It was stated that they did no regular work. Stirner knew these photos and the captions too. They'd been up here for months, and people would stand in front of them, read, look at the photos, because they were waiting for trains that were very late, or they'd missed their connection because their own train had been late, and the waiting room was overcrowded and the station restaurant closed. Stirner heard the woman's voice from the station loudspeaker announce the train for which he was waiting. Platform five.

There were still a few intellectuals who, as in the old days, looked to Paris – but only from force of habit. The connection had been broken, whether or not they were willing to recognize the fact. How many people still studied in Paris then? Who could still travel then? And where to? Wasn't every travel request a war of nerves whose outcome was uncertain? Or which culminated in the fatal letter: It has not been possible to grant your request. Just that. Nothing more. No explanation. Not a word. And that decree that those working in schools or universities were allowed to travel abroad only in the holidays? Of course, there were exceptions: Party ideologue X and the son of Party functionary Y. They were allowed. The few, a little band, soldiered on. They got hold of books and talked about *Tel Quel* and Derrida. And that was all there was to it. What they used to talk about was of interest mainly to the Securitate. The populace would go to the cinema, and if it was an American film, a close-up of Las Vegas by night, or a table laid for breakfast, likewise American, a murmur would run through the aisles. The days of street lighting – they lay so far in the past they were forgotten. And a time when there was still butter on the shelf and pressed ham in the refrigerator (refrigerator, ha ha!) – forgotten. Everybody was preoccupied with getting through the current day. Catching the tram, not having to travel on the running-board, putting in their day's work, the cold, the heat, managing to buy a fresh loaf, perhaps even half a kilo of sausage, not falling ill, having the kid but for what. Those were the nightmares. From Bucharest arrived laws and alterations to laws, written and verbal commands, confidential and secret, decrees and decrees altering decrees, whole waves of instructions came from Bucharest, occupied your mind, orders, nonsense. Kept your mind busy till it moved now only within their limits. This was the oriental aggression which killed all independent thought.

A girl was walking in front of him eating candyfloss. She had a provocative walk. Her legs were short, but she had the walk of a long-legged girl. She was wearing brown slacks. The slacks were old. They gave off a greasy sheen. He could see the stitches of the seam at the rear. Nothing could be seen of the girl's face, except the look of the man who was coming in the opposite direction.

Dear comrades and friends, Stirner shouted. It is more than ever necessary to do everything in our power to reinforce the international solidarity and collaboration of all those – he drained the glass at a gulp – who, he shouted, hold life and peace dear. (Loud applause.) To put an end to the arms race, to defend mankind's supreme vital right to existence, to life, to freedom, to independence and to peace. (In unison: We shall work and we shall fight – and we shall defend peace!) Stirner swayed. He went to the bar. Another glass, he called out, his voice didn't sound loud enough to him. He's got somebody, he heard a voice beside him say. He found himself back at the rostrum, the glass in front of him. He's screwing somebody, said the voice. Was it a woman or a man. He's never at home. I've seen him with her. (Vigorous applause.) Life and experience prove. Stirner reached for the glass. Just now, though, someone else had been standing there opposite him. Creating the conditions for peace and freedom. He wants the kid. He gives the kid money. Steals it, so he said. We are extremely concerned about the situation in the Near East. Fire has broken out in several taverns in the recent period. In every case, the fire brigade managed in time to check and extinguish the blaze. She's got herself an Arab. He's a student. Said he'd marry her. Her parents are against it. She's not allowed out. Stirner clinked glasses with someone. The glass was still half full. The hooligan must answer to the courts for his behaviour. She just vanished from the village, but they managed to trace her. (Loud applause, cheers.) The participants in the discussion expressed their feelings of utmost esteem and gratitude. They decided to have a kid. Then her parents would have to agree. What else could they do? A Gypsy woman came into the bar. Pills for a month, fifty Lei, she called out. Cheaper than schnapps. She's dirty, from Moldavia, ugly. And the poor fool's supporting her. She said she was pregnant. He gave her money. But she wasn't pregnant. He believed she was pregnant though. After serving a number of prison

105

sentences, he was still not doing an honest day's work and even inveigled yet another under-age girl into joining him. So the two of them would hang about in the vicinity of apartment blocks, break into the yards and grab the laundry drying on the lines. She was released from prison, on probation, only in June. She performed the operation on an under-age girl who was already in her eighth month of pregnancy. Stirner held his head in his hands. There were voices in his head. She says he fucks her three times a day. Children, the flowers of life, the spring of our nation. (Cheers and loud applause.) Citizens and citizenesses! They stopped off in Station Square for a little glass of something. The malefactor was arrested. Now he has another meeting. Possibly certain foreign observers may wonder or ask: What kind of democracy can this be, when all decisions are approved unanimously? The Principal fucks the teacher in the school medical room. Anyone who refuses to fuck won't get her job back next year. The notorious criminal has already broken the law more than a hundred times. The young girl wanted to meet a foreigner. There was a dim light in the bar. The smoke hurt Stirner's eyes. He drank. They spent an evening full of love and hope together with friends. Next afternoon they decided to meet on the Maros Promenade. There were fresh declarations of love, of which she understood only a little. At about midnight, as they were admiring the stars on a bench in the Town Park, Roberto suddenly snatched the two gold chains from around her neck and vanished into the darkness with them. But he was soon traced by the militia and identified too. He turned out to be a notorious work-shy character. (Loud, prolonged applause.) Our nation consists of friendly social classes and categories, who have common interests. Stirner fetched himself a new glass. We have approved a splendid programme. We are constantly reinforcing the leading role of the Party, the leading political force of our socialist nation. We have a sure guide – and that is scientific socialism, dialectical materialism, the programme of our Party. Stirner held the glass in his hand. The wine in the glass was swaying. There was a feeling in his head that was stronger than any thought. Both of them must now answer for their crime. Here too she filched various articles of value, until the militia picked up her trail and put a stop to her game. A group of young persons from Pankota was sentenced to terms of imprisonment for their parasitic way of life. At home, where you're needed. He talks just like his father. There's no place like home. We skip round the ram on the village green. Visitors come just like in the old days, but there isn't a costume procession any longer, there aren't enough young people for that. Shit paper, said Stirner. Power from the happiness of others. The community united by tradition. She is an open, obliging person. Throughout the years she has shown great organizational capabilities. She has a sense for tradition and custom, she likes to be involved in everything that happens in her community. Stirner put the newspaper away. We're little people. What can we do after all. The high-ups. There was another fellow there now, stood at the table opposite him, had a glass in front of him, or did he know him from somewhere, was it some old acquaintance, a childhood friend, or the fellow from just now. The fellow raised his index finger. They decide it all up there, over our heads. With his hand he pointed over his head. He held his hand over his head. They do whatever they want. As they like, what they like, anything they like, Stirner mumbled. Next to him someone belched. And what are the writers writing? You're a writer aren't you? What do you think's wrong in the enterprise? Everybody steals as much as he can. Goods for barter. What can you do with money these days? Nothing. Nothing at all. See these hundreds. Trash. Try buying a kilo of meat. A water-tap's worth more than a hundred-Lei note. You can wipe your arse with your hundred-Lei note, or have a drink. What kind of tricks do you think the boss gets up to? All of them in cahoots. All want something. Don't cough up and you won't get any work either. He spat on the floor. Stirner raised his glass. *La multzi ani*, beloved leader, he shouted out to the room. His voice was drowned in the clamour. The writers, totally unanimous in thought and feeling, give expression to their full approval for the ideas, impregnated with a sense of responsibility and with revolutionary pathos, that you formulated during the meeting you held recently with central Party and State activists. Why should I go home. What would I do at home. She'd only fill my ears all over again with it all, you see, her everlasting stories, the same old tune. And then I'd have to beat her. I'm staying here. Closing time, that's me. Who was talking there? Who's talking then? Hey, who's talking here? What do you all want? Leave him be. Shut up. Contemporaries with the future. They promised us a new flat. We were already right at the top of the waiting list. But then somebody else got the flat. Had better connections. (Loud, prolonged applause.) Veterans, just a word! Three decades behind the shop counter. There aren't any white toilet-seats. Bread? Your identity papers. Suck my cock. What are they doling out here, then? Chocolate, I think. Two bars per person. (Cheers and loud applause.) Stirner cast a glance at the shelf. Another bottle, he said, otherwise it'll be time. The shelf was almost empty. Intoxicated and without a driving licence. Drugged and robbed. We're not admitting defeat, come what may. Even if the Turks come, or the Russians, or the rest of them. He fucked me all night long. I think my ribs are broken. Her faulty development commenced, in fact, as soon as she was out of her parents' control – or that of her school or her colleagues at work either. The fact that alcohol also played a part in it cannot justify the crime, or repair the shock which the victim, a mother of two young children, has suffered. Stirner was talking to someone. He didn't give a toss to whom. He was talking to no one. He was talking to himself. Or was he reading? Had he still got those damned newspapers in his hand? He didn't give a toss about himself.

108

Meant nothing to him. Talk came out of him. Was he still in the bar? There was talk everywere. Everywhere. My nephew has a colour television. I'm telling you, the fellow's face is all blotches, he won't last much longer. The President was meant. Oh, he'll live for ever. It's the autumn of the patriarch, anyhow. The tests were continued. This is the eleventh time he will be going to prison. The motive was revenge. A smouldering Kent cost the seventeen-year-old his life. Six illegal abortions could be proved against her. It seemed to Stirner as though he were holding a glass in his hand, a tiny little one, you could barely see it. He lifted it to his mouth, but it vanished. What are the dangers for literature today? There it was again. Dishonesty, evasion of the real problems of our society, illusion, retreat into explanations, excuses, God, those never-ending explanations. Necessary, what's necessary then. Nothing, no crime. Mediocrity, the perversion of criteria and judgement. Balkanism, self-satisfaction. We shouldn't be satisfied. The truth must be spoken. The truth about people and society. (Loud applause and cheers. In unison: Disarmament – Peace! In an atmosphere of strong and enthusiastic unity, all those present rise from their seats and enthusiastically deliver an ovation lasting for several minutes.) While still a child he became acquainted with the difficult situation of the working class under the bourgeois landowning order. As a consequence, he joined the revolutionary movement early on. Because of his participation in various actions in Arad, Temesvar and Resita, he was arrested and sentenced by the organs of repression. After the twenty-third of August nineteen hundred and forty-four, he carried out the Party and State tasks entrusted to him with Communist devotion. For his services he was decorated with orders and medals. The funeral will take place today, at sixteen hours, in the cemetery on Lippa Street. Suddenly Stirner felt the silence. He was standing alone on Station Square. It was dark. Pitch dark. There wasn't a soul to be seen. Hey, he shouted. The

109

echo came back. He shrugged his shoulders, turned round. He looked at the shining tramlines. He began to walk. Along the lines.

And then the day came, it was at the beginning of December. Sabine and Stirner had reflected enough. They'd pondered long enough, they said. They'd endured it long enough. Sabine was thirty-three, Stirner a year older. It was morning. They'd had breakfast. There was no sense in it. The sun was shining over the stadium yonder. There'd been no sense in it for a long time already. Soon it'll be cold again. And the next sickening winter is on its way, and the next sickening speeches by the President are on their way, the next deprivation is on its way, the next weeks without milk are on their way, the days without bread, the evenings without electricity, the next load of media garbage is on its way, the next checking of papers, the next humiliation and the one after that. It was enough. Stirner gazed over the stadium. Behind it lay the dourly smoking industry. The silent countryside. He stood up, went to the cupboard, lifted the typewriter onto the table, laid the lid to one side, inserted two sheets of paper, a carbon in between, began to type: To the Passport Office. We herewith submit our application to emigrate permanently. Our reasons are.

Other fiction titles published by Verso

Saints and Scholars
Terry Eagleton

'. . . ingenious, erudite and entertaining.'
The Times Literary Supplement

Kingdom's End and Other Stories
Saadat Hasan Manto

'. . . superb portaits of the people of his country . . .'
Time Out

The Town Park
Hermann Grab

'. . . deserves to be recognised as one
of the best German short novels of
the century.'
The Times Literary Supplement

Men of Maize
Miguel Angel Asturias

'. . . the fountainhead and the backbone of all
that is being written in our continent today.'
Ariel Dorfman

Field of Honour
Max Aub

'One of the masters of twentieth-century
Spanish prose.'
Emir Rodriguez Monegal

The Conspiracy
Paul Nizan

*With an Afterword by
Jean-Paul Sartre*

The Unseen
Nanni Balestrini

'Lucid, poetic, unforgettable . . .
La Stampa

.